Siren's Serenade

Wiccan Haus
Book 4

By
Dominique Eastwick

Praise for *Siren's Serenade*

Siren's Serenade is spellbinding from the first words.
~ The Bibliophilic Book Blog

I've said this before in another review I wrote here for Hunting J.C. *by Ms. Eastwick, but I will admit freely that I am addicted to her stories! Her Wiccan Haus characters are excellent and her twists and turns keep me riveted. I was quite pleased she didn't give us stereotypical mermaids and Paras and I actually thought Kaleb was an awesome hero! I always keep my eyes open for Ms. Eastwick's work and for the next addition to this series* ~The Romance Studio

In the fourth book of the multi-author Wiccan Haus series, Dominique Eastwick brings the reader a sweet love story filled with more plot twists than ocean currents in the sea. ~ Sensual Reads

Don't miss this beautiful sea glass gem. Siren's Serenade is richly colored and spellbinding. I hope you will be as drawn in as I was. I would suggest that you read the prior books in the series first though. Without them you will not understand why I enjoyed this book so much. While it is not completely necessary, you minus well dive right in and get caught up in the storm. The Wiccan Haus series is a treasure that needs to be enjoyed to its fullest! ~Books Read and MakeUp Done

The plot is solid and exciting, the sex is hot and the

characters are to die for. ~ Amazon Reviewer

Ms. Eastwick writes such a wonderful story filled with paranormal creatures and magic that I'm dying to visit Wiccan Haus for myself. ~ Amazon Reviewer

If you're a lover of paranormal, I totally recommend this series and Ms. Eastwick. ~ Amazon Reviewer

Another wonderful paranormal story by Dominique Eastwick. I can't wait to get back to the Wiccan Haus! ~ Amazon Reviewer

This is a very very must read at 5 stars. ~ Amazon Reviewer

The story line was wonderful and is one not to be missed! I loved, loved, loved, this story! I've struggled trying to find any helpful criticism but I'm at a loss for even one. This is a story I would thoroughly recommend to any lover of paranormal, romance, military or simply a great read. This for me was flawless! ~ Amazon Reviewer

~A Letter from Dominique~

The Wiccan Haus series is so close to my heart. Rekkus has quickly become my favorite character I have written and nothing makes me more excited than seeing how other authors work him and all the siblings into their books. And as much as I wanted to write another story all about Rekkus and Dana, the resident mermaid informed me it was her turn so sit back, relax and welcome back to the Wiccan Haus.

Dedication

To all my Wiccan Haus sisters who help to make the Wiccan Haus a place I would want to stay at. Dedicated to Tina B., T.t., Star, Delphina, Trish, and Toni the fans who inspire us to write more books in the series.

Special thanks to Liz, Kate, Sara, Nya, Carolyn, and Rebecca for helping to bring this world to life. And for loving the island and its inhabitants as much as I do.

As always, to Nadine and last but not least, my hubby

Prologue

Serena didn't dare face her mother. Either she would tell her matriarch off, laugh in her face—or, worse, burst into a sea of tears. The final would be a humiliation she couldn't quite deal with. For the last two centuries, Serena had listened to her mother lament to their chorus of mermaids how incompetent and embarrassing her middle daughter proved as both an heir apparent and a mermaid.

True, Serena hadn't done her duty to either her queen or her people. She had failed to secure the line of succession. Serena didn't understand why, but when she was born, the old sea hag had declared she would be the strength of her people. *She* would bring about change, and *she* would succeed to the throne. Serena had long ago decided someone had misheard. Serena would never be the strength of anyone and didn't see why the old woman of the sea had the power to decide who would be next on the throne. She certainly hadn't shown the strength her people thought she should have when she'd helped those shipwrecked men out of the watery depths.

"This is the last time you will embarrass me." Her mother's voice boomed through the cavernous throne room.

"I can't kill a man whose only sin is being a *man*." Serena looked at her mother and wished she hadn't; her striking beauty became cold and harsh.

"They pollute our waters, rape our food source, and you can't protect your people by dragging the few worthy specimens to us so we can mate?"

"Not when mating with them means they shall take their last breath!" Having known the pleasure of para men on more than one occasion, Serena had yet to understand why her mother and sisters were so keen on seeing any man die after giving a mermaid what she wanted. "I will find a man on land and mate with him, but I will not kill one."

"You have one year from this day to do just that. You *will* secure the line, or we'll force the mating on you, Serena. Do what you have to, but you had better be with child by this time next year."

"I can't."

"You will. Do not defy me on this." Her mother snubbed her, in a show of passive-aggressiveness she spun away, flipping her tail forward and away from Serena.

Gasping, Serena understood the meaning. When a mermaid did this, the recipient of the gesture was no longer worthy of her attention. For all intents and purposes, she'd been cast out until she fulfilled her destiny. Serena barely paid heed to her sisters turning tail from her as well. Not one of them had the scales to stand up to their mother.

With all the power she possessed, Serena kicked out of the great hall and toward the surface. Moving faster and faster, she focused on the sun's light twinkling above her. Cresting, she threw her long blonde hair back with a flick of her head, tresses drying as they hit the air. And then, she let her anger mount. She hit the ocean surface with her fist and screamed with all the sorrow her soul allowed. She wanted to sing, but any sailors in the area would succumb to her sorrow.

"Serena." The whisper seemed to come on the breeze. Her eldest sister broke the water's barrier. Unlike her, Serafina had never enjoyed the air or the sun. Taking Serena's wrist, Serafina dragged her back down into the depths into a cave they had played in as girls. Coming out of the water into the dark recesses of the cave, Serena followed her sister to the area lit with pools of bioluminescent fish. "There is a place run by other paras. They might be able to help you."

Serena pulled free. What hope did she have if even the meekest of sisters couldn't be on her side even in private? "Help me kill someone?"

"No. Help you break the curse that forces us to kill a man to get with child."

Moving to the clear pool in the center of the cave, Serafina ran her fingers through the water. The image of a small island appeared in the pool. "They heal people. Perhaps they can heal you or at least help you to find peace with your destiny."

"I want nothing to do with this destiny."

"You have very little choice, my sister. This place can help. I just know it. It's called the Wiccan

Haus."

Chapter One

One Year Later

"Sign…again." Rekkus, head of security for the Wiccan Haus, placed back into her palm the pen designed by Sarka, one of the Wiccan Haus owners, to bind Serena to her promise.

Damn him. Why couldn't he take her for her word? Just once? So maybe she'd given him reason to doubt her on an occasion or two, but no one had been hurt. Not really. But the tall, dark brooding man before her didn't take anyone at their word. And that made him so good at his job. It also added to his appeal.

Oh, what she wouldn't give to get that cat into her pond one more time.

"Damn it, Serena, sign. The humans are arriving any minute, and I don't have time for your games."

She slammed the pen against the paper, causing the ink to splotch, sucking in her breath as the metal burned her fingertips. Without reading the document,

Serena signed her name, yanked a hair from her head, and placed it in its envelope. "Happy?"

"Fucking ecstatic." Rekkus snatched it up before disappearing into the office behind the desk. No man—human or para—should fill out a pair of jeans the way he did. And she knew what those jeans held, too.

"Welcome back, Serena."

Shit. She closed her eyes. Bad form checking out a man when his mate stood right there. "Hello, Dana." Serena held no ill will against the human woman who had captured not only the tiger's heart but his soul. But that didn't mean she couldn't replay the sex with him in her head.

"He does wear those jeans well, doesn't he?"

"I wasn't looking. I was just…."

"You were. Everyone does. But then, who am I to blame you?" Dana leaned toward Serena, whispering in her ear. "It's okay, you know. I'm not the jealous type."

"Why are you so nice to me?"

Shrugging, Dana laughed. "Because I can be.

7

Maybe, this time, you'll find whatever peace has eluded you." She followed Rekkus into the office.

What about Dana made her so damned nice? No one except Serena's older sister was ever nice to her for no reason. Hell, even when Serena had been fucking Rekkus, he hadn't been nice to her. That had been two paras slaking their lust. Sex didn't mean the same to paras as it did to humans, or so she had begun to understand.

Still, the issue of trust gnawed at her. How did a mermaid, who put faith in no one, get people to trust her? And why did it matter so much to her anyway?

On her second visit, she'd overheard Myron the receptionist say to Rekkus that she couldn't read her with her cards. That she had tried several decks, but none read the same. When Rekkus had questioned her, Myron shrugged and explained that mermaids were never truthful even to themselves, so how could the cards read her intent when she didn't even know it?

And that was the crux of the issue.

Serena had spent years fighting her instinct as a

mermaid to bring human men to their doom. So, what did someone who couldn't embrace her true self, pretending to be anything else, become in the end?

"Serena, I have you in one of the cabins this week. As we weren't expecting you, your usual room was given to a were-shark in need of the salt-water bath."

"Thanks, Myron. It's fine."

"Sage said to tell you she will be down to infuse the cabin later. There isn't a bath, but it's right on the beach, so you should be fine. A word of warning: it's damn close to Rekkus and Dana. And, aside from them being rather loud, if you catch my meaning, if a human sees your…um…fin, Rekkus will blow his already volatile top. He is, to put it bluntly, a walking time bomb, and no one is quite sure why. Not even me." The gypsy placed her cards one at a time on the table then scrunched her nose at the results.

"Well warned, thank you." Serena gave a weak smile, grabbed her key from Myron, and walked down the path to the beach. She heard the ferry approaching but couldn't be bothered to watch the humans disembark. She couldn't imagine a human having anything that would interest her anyway. She had hours before dinner. Maybe luck would be kind to her and, when all the humans were drugged into sleep while the portal opened to let the other paras into the Wiccan Haus, she could fit in a swim. Maybe she could find the peace Dana had pointed out had so far eluded her.

Time, after all, was not on her side. She was hiding. Even Myron's cards would have read that, had she bothered to flip them.

***

Kaleb regarded the distance between the ferry and the dock coming into sight. Having emerged from the thickest wall of fog he had ever seen—and in his career he had seen a lot of fog—his alert senses knew something about this place seemed off. Glancing at his watch, he tapped it once before bringing it to his ear to make sure it ticked. He had corrected the time when he landed in Bangor the night before, but the sun's position in the sky didn't make sense. But, then again, maybe he was just as crazy as all his Coast Guard buddies thought. Even if they *were* calling it post-traumatic stress disorder.

Maybe they were right. The stress of watching his best friend die before his eyes and not being able to rescue him had made him a bit nuts for a while. Kaleb had been right there, inches away as Jim had been dragged under. Not by a wave or a shark—no, that would be par for the course—but by *something* Kaleb wasn't willing to say ever again, not even to himself. He'd said it in his shock to those on the helicopter when he had been lifted up, and then to the shrink when his buddies reported it to the master chief.

And this is where it had landed him.

Kaleb grabbed his duffle bag, threw it over his shoulder, and waited while the couples disembarked. He offered to carry the bag of a woman with a bad limp, but a member of the staff lifted it and started off. He focused on the swinging sign that said in big, bold gold letters: *The Wiccan Haus*.

Unbelievable. You tell a shrink you see a mermaid luring your best friend to his death, and they send you to a spa of spiritual healing run by witches. And they called me *crazy.* Kaleb shook his head.

Walking into the large, airy lobby, he waited patiently in line. Security men surveyed everyone as they entered, and Kaleb wondered why a spa needed so much muscle. These guys could have rivaled the Secret Service with the exception of a suit. These guys all wore black jeans, a black T-shirt, and black combat boots. They had the air of someone protecting the president complete with earpieces.

"Good afternoon, and welcome to the Wiccan Haus. You must be Kaleb Theldon." The woman behind the desk smiled at him, flipped a few cards in her solitaire game then slid him a key. "You're in room three, third floor, third elevator. Hmm that's a lot of threes," she murmured, shrugged, and then passed him a folder. "Here is a list of required classes for you. Hopefully, they can assist in your healing."

"Sage—"

"It's Myron. I can't find my name tag." She

smiled. "*Again.*"

"Myron, unless you can heal crazy, I doubt these classes will be of any help."

"Oh, you're not crazy, Petty Officer Theldon." Myron flipped a last card and turned it crossways above the center card. Staring at the three of hearts, she peered at him through lowered eyelashes. "Hmm, another three. No, not crazy in the least. Enjoy your stay…. Hello, welcome back to the Wiccan Haus, Ms. Shanis."

Having been dismissed by the rather flaky Myron, Kaleb took a deep breath and headed past the giant who stood guard over the second elevator as if it held national secrets and made his way to the third elevator. The security guards here made *him* appear small. Kaleb waited next to four others for the lift doors to open. His fellow guests chatted, and he smiled at them. It seemed as if everyone else was here of their own free will, while he had been dragged by force. He would do as he had been ordered: take his classes and vow never to mention what he had seen. Anything to get approved for active duty again, back to the job he loved and the team he thought of as family.

A sense of calm came over him as he walked into his room. Though small, the room didn't feel claustrophobic, and with the dark-wood king-sized bed in the center of the white-walled room, it had a homey feel. Dropping his duffle bag on the leather armchair in the corner, Kaleb walked to a little alcove of natural wood at the far end of the room and opened the window wide. The view of the ocean took his breath away, and although he hadn't requested a beachside room, he was thankful nonetheless for the cadence of the waves as they lapped the shore.

Exhaustion overtook him. Perhaps the stress of the last few weeks caught up with him, but for the first time since that dreadful storm, Kaleb let himself stop thinking. Determined to only rest his eyes, he toed his shoes off and lay down on the large bed. He listened to the ocean and breathed in the deep, clean air surrounding him. Exhaustion turned to relief as sleep overcame him, and he had no desire to fight it off.

He awoke to a loud knocking on his door. Glancing at his watch, he was shocked he had slept several hours. Yawning, he shook the edges of sleep off and threw his legs over the side of the bed, gathering his bearings. Only as the knock became more persistent and louder did he get to his feet and head to the door.

"What?" he demanded, throwing open the door.

One of the security men he'd observed earlier filled the doorway.

"Dinner is served," he barked. "It's required that everyone on the island attend." The dominant air about the man told Kaleb he must be the head honcho.

"Right. Give me a second to get my shoes, and I'll head down."

The man grunted before marching to the door across the hall and pounding there. "Damn it, Sage," the man muttered.

"Don't mind Rekkus," a blonde bohemian woman said with a grin. "He's always surly."

"I heard that," Rekkus said, banging on yet

another door. Had everyone on the floor decided to nap?

"You were supposed to," the woman said, laughing. "I'm Sage, and you must be…Kaleb?"

"That's me. And you're one of the owners?"

"I am. I hope you found the room comfortable. We try to customize the accommodations to the guests to help in healing."

"Of course he damned well likes it. The whole damned floor liked their rooms so much not one of them came down to dinner," Rekkus said from behind them.

"Surly," Sage said with a wink.

Had Kaleb been in the same position, he would have been just as pissed. He imagined the last thing on the security guard's job description was babysitting a horde of guests and making sure they got to dinner.

"I'm not *surly,* Sage, I am *pissed off* and merely stating you overdid it this time."

"Rekkus, meet Petty Officer Second Class Theldon. Kaleb is a member of Search and Rescue with the Coast Guard."

Rekkus seemed to measure Kaleb before asking, "Why are you here?"

"My superiors think I'm nuts."

Rekkus walked with them into the elevator and waited for it to fill before jabbing a button. "Well, you're in good company. They're all fucking nuts here."

"Rekkus."

"Don't you dare 'Rekkus' me. If you hadn't caused this, I would be—"

"Dana isn't going anywhere, you nutty tiger. Good lord, she even married you."

"Sage, one day you will…."

Kaleb left them in the elevator, certain Sage would win out over the large man. Stomach growling, Kaleb couldn't care less about the squabbling of hotel employees.

In the dining room, he found a heck of a lot more people than he had expected. Only twelve had arrived on the boat with him, and he had been told the boat came once a week. The number of guests in the dining room was more than double that. The group he had arrived with all seemed to have gravitated to the area of the dining room painted light green. There must be some new-age name for the color, but "light green" worked for him. The rest of the people all were in the darker green. He must have missed the memo that said which area his table would be located.

Then he saw *her*, sitting alone in the corner, sipping her soup. The most beautiful woman he had ever seen. Her long blonde hair lay over bare shoulders, caressing barely-covered breasts. His mouth watered as his eyes soaked in the sight of her. Kaleb took a few steps in her direction, but a strange uneasiness came over him as he crossed into the darker-green area. How odd. Nausea increased as he approached her. He paused and took a few steps back, the feeling subsiding with each step. This place got weirder and weirder. He moved back into the light-green side and the uneasiness disappeared. It made his head spin to consider the situation. He had to get through this week, and then maybe, if he kept what he had seen to himself, he would get back to his crew and team and what he excelled at—rescuing people at sea. But, even knowing what was good for him, his gaze still stayed on the blonde in the corner.

"She's not for you, Mr. Theldon. Trust me; her beauty is skin deep."

Kaleb turned to see a tall goth woman standing beside him. Her blue eyes showed no compassion. "And why would you care?"

"I don't. She is not someone, no matter how good a swimmer you are, you should get into deep water with."

"Never mind Sarka," Sage said. "I would say my sister's bark is worse than her bite, but that would be a lie."

"So, I shouldn't stay away from the blonde?"

"Everyone comes to the Wiccan Haus for their own private reasons, Mr. Theldon. That is all I can say about Serena."

Though Sage's words seemed to have a world of meaning, she didn't further explain but placed him at a table with a direct and unhindered view of the blonde woman. Her beauty reminded him of sunset over the ocean. He, a man who had never waxed poetic in his life, saw this woman in sappy terms, all related to the ocean. Perhaps he grew crazier by the minute.

He sat down, and Sage handed him a sheet of paper. "Your schedule for tonight. We had to readjust, due to your nap."

Massage with Lakshmi.

Now, that's more like it. Maybe he would get through this week after all.

Chapter Two

Serena sank into the pond as it sprang to life around her. The water vibrated and hummed with energy. Dropping deep into the water, she checked around before allowing her legs merge into one large fin. She leaned back and let her head float, face above the water. The dusky sky had turned the beautiful color of coral in the Mediterranean, shades of orange and pink blended together in breathtaking splendor. This was her favorite time of day here on the island, when the guests were getting ready for dinner and she had the lake to herself.

Humming, she let the water run her over her skin and scales. Rekkus had been clear: no singing within the perimeter of the island. But he hadn't forbidden her from the rest. Silly tiger. He should have known she could hum a serenade as well as sing. The only difference between the two? Her humming didn't carry far. Perhaps he knew and didn't care.

Her private sessions with Sage and Cemil were

getting her no closer to finding a way to break the curse. Sarka had, as always, been less than helpful, saying she should take down a vampire to mate with. For Serena to procreate, the soul of the man had to enter her babe—and vampires had none.

But she had to either break this curse within a few weeks or her mother would force the breeding on her. And that wouldn't be good for anyone. She had thought about leaving, but nowhere in the ocean's depths could she hide from her mother. Unless Serena could find a saltwater lake high on a mountaintop and someone to fly her to it, her mother would never stop.

She paused, sensing rather than hearing something in the distance. Serena placed her whole head under the water and, with one great thrust of her tail, plunged deep into the lake's recesses to the opening she had discovered months ago that allowed her access to the ocean. A woman in trouble—Serena could hear it in vibrations threading through the water. The woman's fear overcame Serena as she came out of the dark tunnel. She might not get there in time, and she sensed no sea life close enough to help. Serena pushed her powerful tail through the water, closer and closer to the panic.

Damn, the woman needed to calm down before she attracted a shark. And although she sensed a group of porbeagle sharks, as well as a blue shark in the distance, they seemed uninterested in fighting through the barriers of the island to get to a meal. Serena propelled a little farther to ensure that no great whites were passing through the area. She could outrun a great, but not easily while carrying the weight of another.

Nearing the water's edge, she sensed another closing in on the woman. About to fight off whoever stood in her way, Serena stopped. Above her, a man swam with powerful strokes, graceful and determined, muscles rippling in the water, perfection in male form. Serena's body sprang to life like it had never before. But not due to solely the sheer beauty of his body, something Serena never hesitated to admire.

He headed for the victim, with no concern for his own safety, in cold and unforgiving waters. Cresting a few yards from him, Serena watched in silence, her moving tail keeping her in place, as the man maneuvered the woman into his arms. The distressed human fought him at first, forcing him under, but his strength and determination won out. He said something Serena couldn't decipher over the splashing. Had she been underwater, she would have felt the vibrations and understood.

"Can I help?" Surprised to hear her breathless tone, she stopped swimming for a second.

"God, where did you come from?" He jerked around, peering across the whitecaps.

Words caught in her throat as a pair of amber eyes widened in shock. Gorgeous didn't begin to describe the bronze skin tone and well-defined features. His short, dark hair, even wet, framed his face. Careful to stay to the side and fin down, she answered, "I saw you come in to help and thought to lend a hand." Oh, how she wished she could make her tail into legs right now, but her body would never allow the change in this depth.

"I got her. Can you get back to shore and get help?"

"Of course. Swim to the side over there—a strong rip current is this way, and there are cabins on the shore in that direction." Hoping he stayed on his back so he couldn't see her as she headed for land, Serena dove deep again. It was the only way she could beat him back to the shore without giving up her true nature. Swimming below the surface, she made it to land far quicker than she knew any human could. When she hit the beach, her fin split into two legs, and she stumbled—not at all like her normal, graceful self. Moving on unstable feet, Serena reached the door of Rekkus and Dana's cabin. Pounding, she yelled Rekkus's name.

"What is it?" He threw the door open, pulling his pants up, and, for the first time, the sight of a naked Rekkus did nothing for her overactive libido. "Put some clothes on."

Serena took inventory of her naked body and willed the clothes to form around her like a veil. She often wondered at the need to cover up what was natural but knew her nudity made humans uncomfortable, and Rekkus simply didn't want to see it.

"You've got to call for help. A woman got caught in a rip." Serena pointed to the figures coming closer to shore.

"Dana, call for Sage and Cyrus," Rekkus called over his shoulder, racing into the water and stroking out to assist the man.

Dana appeared in the doorway, her curvaceous body barely covered in one of Rekkus's T-shirts. "Sorry, I didn't mean to interrupt. It's…."

Dana grabbed the walkie-talkie and told whoever on the other end what they needed and where. "Serena, you did good, real good. Come on." She threw a few blankets at Serena and grabbed some towels and bottled water.

Serena followed Dana's lead. By the time they reached the shore, Rekkus had lifted the woman out of the water, and the swimmer kneeled on the beach, gasping for breath. Dana threw a towel over the shaking woman.

"Here." Serena handed the blanket to the man. "Come on, let's get you inside."

He nodded, following at a slower pace. As they entered the cottage, Rekkus growled for Dana to get some clothes on. Serena suppressed a giggle as Dana rolled her eyes but obeyed. Rekkus laid the woman on the sofa and tucked a blanket around her. These waters were cold at the best of times, but this early in the season, they were downright chilly.

"Have a seat. Get out of those wet clothes. My mate will get you something dry to wear, and, if I know Sage, she'll be here any minute with some hot tea." Rekkus moved his golden focus to her. "Serena, can you start a fire?"

"No." She had never lit a match in her life, let alone a fire.

About to suggest he do it, she remembered that Rekkus's body temperature ran higher than any human's. By sitting next to the woman they'd rescued, his natural heat would warm her.

"Don't worry. I have it." Dana came out of the bedroom in a sundress complete with hoop skirt and with some running pants and a sweatshirt in her arms. "Mr. Thelon, these are for you. The legs might be a bit long, but they should fit well enough."

"Please, call me Kaleb, and thank you." The human god walked into the bathroom and closed the door. Serena wanted nothing more than to break down the offending door and see this human naked. She nearly fell out of her chair, trying to watch for him to turn the corner.

"Serena, be careful," Rekkus muttered.

"I'm always careful."

Dana choked on what at first seemed to be a laugh but turned into a cough.

Serena blinked at her. "Are you all right?"

"Fine."

"I think Dana is trying to kindly infer that you are the least careful being she has ever met."

"Rekkus!"

"What?"

A new feeling simmered in Serena. Unable to label it, she let it cover her as she watched the were and his mated bride with a smile on her lips. Yet, something in her longed for what Dana had. Not with Rekkus. Although he had been a wonderful lay, he could be as intense as the darkest part of the ocean. Hell, he made her mother seem downright happy.

Kaleb interrupted the banter between the lovers by returning from the bathroom as the same moment Sage and Cyrus barged in the front door. Sage, true to form, held a bowl of steaming hot liquid. She indicated with a jerk of her chin for Cyrus to offer the smaller cup to Kaleb before inching Rekkus out of the way and helping the shivering woman bring the bowl to her lips.

Rekkus walked to the far wall and talked in undertones to Cyrus. Both men focused on Serena for a second before returning to the group.

"We can't thank you enough for rescuing Ms. Davis as you did," Sage said with a kind smile to Kaleb.

"It's what I do," he said, his voice betraying no sense of pride or heroism, as if it were a matter of fact.

"Nonetheless, we are thankful. These waters aren't often susceptible to riptides, and had you not been there, our guest would not be here." Cyrus removed his glove and shook hands with the human.

What the...? Cyrus never removed his gloves unless trying to read someone.

And, a second later, her suspicions were confirmed when, reaching for the mug Kaleb had been drinking out of, he paused before asking, "Serena, may Rekkus and I speak to you for a moment?"

Serena nodded and followed the two outside, sure they had found some reason to blame this all on her. After all, Dana might have said she had done well, but no one else would believe that of a mermaid.

Once outside, and, she assumed, out of earshot of those inside the building, Rekkus turned and asked, "Are you sure it was a riptide?"

"It felt like one to me."

Rekkus stared out at the ocean, which seemed as calm now as he was tense, his clenched fists resting on his hips. "Serena, you sensed nothing out there?"

"Sorry, no. I focused on the girl. But he got there first." Serena closed her eyes and envisioned those strong arms and legs slicing through the water.

"Serena, concentrate. What did you sense in the water? Think past the fear coming off Ms. Davis."

With Cyrus's gloved fingers on her shoulder, she normally would have been flirting her tail off. The warlock never touched her, no matter how hard she had tried to get his attention. Yet, his touch did nothing but return her thoughts to the matter before them—the strange tides invading the area. What had been around her? She thought she had sensed some fish, those few sharks, but nothing paranormal. Definitely not her mother or any of her kind. "Nothing. I sensed there were some sharks, but no one else close by."

Kaleb watched Serena walk out of the cottage with the two men following close behind. Dana headed into the kitchen as Sage continued to comfort the shivering woman by rubbing her shoulders.

Nothing made sense in this place. Rekkus—granted, a man in great shape—had lifted Ms. Davis out of the water like she weighed nothing. And who the hell referred to their wife as their mate? Not to mention the inhuman sound the man made when he asked his "mate" to change clothes.

As his head cleared, his chill driven away with dry clothes and warm tea, Kaleb remembered even more things that didn't make sense. Serena, the beauty, had swum faster than anyone he had ever met. She had managed to outswim him through a riptide, reach the shore, get dressed, and return with help before he had made it a hundred yards. But, thanks to her, the girl on the sofa—whose blue color had worried him—wore a healthier glow of rosy pink.

Added to the large nature and muscular build of all the security men on the island, Kaleb wondered if perhaps this crazy spa wasn't full of steroid users as well. Nothing else made any sense, and it meant he had to be ultra-careful about what he ate and took.

Moving to the door, he listened in as the two men talked with Serena.

"Serena, you sensed nothing out there?"

"Sorry, no. I focused on the girl. But he got there first."

Kaleb peeked through the open doorway. Rekkus

growled, and Cyrus touched Serena's bare shoulder. An unreasonable sense of jealousy came over Kaleb. "Serena, concentrate. What did you sense in the water? Think past the fear coming off Ms. Davis."

"Nothing. I sensed there were some sharks, but no one else close by."

"You will tell me immediately if you sense anything."

"Good Goddess, Rekkus. You know I will."

"I know you better than most. That's what I know." Rekkus moved away from the couple. He paced, catlike, at the water's edge.

"What did I do this time?" Serena's small voice made her seem fragile.

"What does anyone have to do right now to set him off?" Cyrus said with a shrug. "But, as you already know, it isn't in his nature to trust, and you still have to make up for the concert you gave the last time you were here."

"It was one little song,"

"Where you are concerned, there is no 'little song' about it."

She sighed, looking at Rekkus. "I did apologize."

"That might have been the least heartfelt apology in history. But you came a long way today in making up for that escapade." Cryus paused, staring at the other man. "I'm going to see what is going on in that cunning brain of his."

"Better you than me."

"You can say that again."

Serena tilted her head. "Better you than me."

Cyrus laughed, patting her shoulder before walking away. "It's a saying, Serena. You didn't have to repeat it."

"But...."

Watching the lower lip protrude from her mouth in a beautiful pout, Kaleb felt his cock harden. He cursed the running pants that did nothing to conceal his present state. With the blood leaving his brain for parts far lower, he had a hard time focusing on the conversation that had happened. Nothing about it made sense. But perhaps things were not what they seemed. She said she had not *sensed* anything in the water—perhaps she had jumped from a small raft to see if she could help. No, he would have seen a boat. She could have been on shore, maybe working with sonar, when the other woman got into trouble. That could explain her arriving on the scene and the speed she had going back if she hadn't fought the rip current to begin with.

"Thank you for saving her." Her voice floated over him like the ocean breeze.

Obviously, he wasn't a very good spy. Stepping out of the doorway, Kaleb shrugged and gave his standard answer, uncomfortable with hero worship. "It's what I do."

She cocked her head to the left, as if confused by his statement and trying to work it out in her mind. Her voice held a hint of an accent, but he couldn't place it—not that he knew anything about dialects. Kaleb was lucky he could tell the difference from Alaskans and Texans.

"I rescue people for a living. I'm a rescue swimmer with the Coast Guard."

"Ah. You ride in one of the big white boats?"

"No, actually I am assigned to a helicopter. Or

was."

"Helicopter?"

This time, he tilted his head to the side. "You know, a helicopter, flies in the air, can hover above the land or water?"

"Oh, right." She smiled and laughed, making him almost forget their strange conversation. "Not every man would have helped her, so thank you."

"If I hadn't been there, you would have managed on your own. I've never met a swimmer as fast as you. Were you an Olympian?"

"Olympus would never have me." She squinched her nose as if thinking about it. "My mother would say I learned to swim before I could stand."

"Crawl...the saying is swam before you learned to crawl."

"That, too." Again with the smile. Damn, this woman hit him right in the solar plexus.

"So, what's the verdict, Cyrus?" Sage asked, coming from the cabin with Ms. Davis. Dana helped Sage escort the woman to the waiting golf cart.

Cyrus murmured something else to Rekkus

before turning to his sibling. "No one senses anything. Probably just a freak rip current. We'll keep an eye on it."

"Well then, as long as everyone stays close to shore, we should be all set. Dinner is being served." She turned to Kaleb and Serena. "Do you two want a ride, or would you prefer to walk?"

Serena waited. Like her decision hinged on his. "I think I'll walk."

"Me, too."

"Excellent," Sage answered before yelling for Cyrus who returned from the water's edge.

Rekkus's reaction, a near-growl, brought Kaleb up short—the second time he had made that inhuman sound. "It's not excellent, damn it. Sage, you knock it off. Serena, I'm warning you."

"Consider me warned. I am on my best behavior."

Had Kaleb not been walking so close to them, he would have missed the "You'd better be."

"Dana, please do something with your mate," Sage said with a laugh.

"I try, but even I have my limits."

"I'm right here, ladies," Rekkus grumbled before letting Dana lure him back into the cabin.

Climbing behind the wheel of the golf cart, Sage winked at them. "Ignore Rekkus. It's good for him to not have someone jump at his commands. Okay, you two, see you up in the main dining room in twenty minutes. Please don't make Rekkus track you down. It won't go well for anyone, especially me."

Kaleb's determination to discover The Wiccan Haus's secrets doubled. If his body would let him focus on anything other than the goddess next to him.

"So, do you work here, or are you a guest?" Kaleb asked when they were finally alone.

"I'm a regular guest here. This is my fifth visit to the Haus."

"Fifth?" He didn't want to be here once, and she'd come back for a fifth visit?

"Yes."

"Wow, and you're here because you want to be?"

"Of course. Aren't you?"

"I was ordered here."

Serena stopped walking. "Ordered by whom?"

"My superiors."

She sighed. The action filled her lungs and lifted her breasts. Kaleb's fingers itched to reach up and touch her. The lust she created in him with a simple look or small sound from those lips drove him insane. He could not remember ever wanting someone this much. It wasn't only her beauty or her sex appeal. He couldn't put his finger on it.

"My superior is the reason I'm here, too, but somehow I doubt your superior is your mother."

"Um no, and if I called him that, I'd find myself scrubbing toilets with a toothbrush."

"Why would you do that?"

"That is the ultimate question." He chuckled, moving toward the Haus as it came into sight through the trees. "Would you like to join me for dinner?"

"Yes." No delay, no thought, just a simple yes.

"Okay, let me go change. I'll meet you in the lobby in ten."

"Ten?"

"Ten minutes? Where are you from?"

She blushed then turned away. "My home is a bit secluded."

He rubbed his palms together, stalling for time. He didn't want to leave but did want to get into his own clothes. "Be right back."

Serena bit her lip and watched him jog away. Kaleb was like no one she had ever met. She'd had very little interaction with humans—men especially, for the obvious reasons—but she couldn't stay away from this one. He pulled her like a Siren's song. She wondered if this was the effect her singing had on men. The inability to think clearly, the desire to be close? Moving up to the main desk, she rang the bell. When no one came, she rang again.

"Serena?" Myron came out of the main office, eating an apple.

"Myron, what's a *helicopter?*"

The gypsy paused. "Helicopter?"

"You don't know either?"

"Of course I know, but why the sudden interest in flying machines?"

"Please, can you tell me?"

"Come around here. It's better if I show you."

Serena had never been behind the desk before. She had seen people sitting at the funny box Myron took her to but didn't know what it was or why anyone could find it so interesting.

"If you're asking about helicopters, I assume you are interested in Kaleb, our Coast Guard hottie."

She nodded. Just thinking about him made her mouth go dry. With a few clicks of the bright-colored shell-like item on the desk, a moving picture of a flying machine appeared on the box. "He jumps from those?"

"I gather."

Serena watched the *videos,* as Myron called them, so enthralled with what the Coast Guard did, she didn't notice Kaleb coming back. "You ready for dinner?"

Moving her attention from the *computer*, Serena smiled. Nodding, she got up but stopped when Myron pursed her lips. "My cards can read you."

"What?"

"I can read you with my cards."

"What are they saying?"

"Stay away from the lake."

Serena grimaced. "Is that the cards or Rekkus speaking?"

Myron placed the cards again. "It's the cards, though Rekkus would say the same thing."

"Very well."

"Really. Stay away from the lake. Oh, and have fun."

What did she mean? Serena squinted at the gypsy's face but couldn't understand why the woman would be smiling. Walking around the desk, Serena took the hand Kaleb offered her. Her fingers touched his warm, rough ones, and a shimmer of electricity ran down her spine. "No one's ever asked me to join them for dinner before."

"You must be joking."

"No, that isn't a joke. I always eat alone." No one would eat with her. The vamps wanted nothing to do with her. The shifters, once they had smelled Rekkus's scent on her, had backed away, assuming the alpha on the island had laid his claim. And, although he hadn't, she had been secretly relieved to be left alone. She didn't enjoy having the shifters sniff her out. The few elves, changelings, and fae on the island when she visited had such a deep-seated hatred of the merfolk they had been downright rude in their interactions. Not that she blamed them. Ever since the mermen had disappeared, leaving the mermaids to take lives to procreate, only vampires were spared the mermaids' songs.

The humans, though interested, had been unable to cross the dark-green section of the dining room. Which left her to eat alone. Because, although humans might not know what she was, a para could sense her a league away.

"The men here must be blind or stupid." Lifting her hand to his mouth, Kaleb kissed her knuckles. The odd gesture left her short of breath.

They were late as they entered the full dining room, but there had been no way to prevent it. Serena had been willing to risk the wrath of Sarka to rescue the woman. No wrath in sight, though, Serena wondered how she would be able to eat with this strange lump in her throat.

The wait staff didn't even blink when they brought her meal to her. She ate her fish raw, but tonight, they had disguised her usual fare as something they called *sushi*. And she had to admit, she found it delicious.

"What I wouldn't give for a steak," Kaleb muttered, poking the green leaves on his plate with his fork.

"Why not order one? I know Rekkus has steaks brought to the island for the shif— for the Shifter brothers."

"I was informed I need to 'clear my auras and cleanse my inner being.'"

"Oh?"

"Yeah. Not sure how much of this green shit I can take."

"You want some of my sushi?" she offered.

"No offense, but no, thank you. I would rather drink one of Sage's shakes than eat that." He wrinkled his nose, such a cute and out of place expression on his handsome face, she couldn't help but laugh.

"Come on and try it. It's quite delicious." She lifted the seaweed wrap to his lips. "What are you, duck?"

"Duck? I think you mean 'chicken,' and, no, I like my meat cooked."

"Your loss." She smiled, shoving the whole piece into her mouth with glee.

"What class do you have tonight?"

"I don't take classes. I have private meetings with the siblings when they say I need to." She didn't add that the reason had to do with her singing in one of those classes. The charm had taken days to wear off.

"How did you get that lucky? I have to see Trixie. She's supposed to teach me to breathe. I guarantee you *that* is something I've never had trouble with." He took another bite of salad. "Come with me."

"To class? I can't, but I would love to meet you after." Serena wanted to get back on that computer.

She needed to know more about his world—for instance, where he lived.

"It's a date."

Serena smiled and vowed to ask Myron what a date was.

Chapter Three

Breathing class went about as well as Kaleb thought it would. He couldn't get into the whole *find your chi* thing, and finding his inner self. His inner self said he wasn't crazy. He knew what he'd seen. No matter what anyone else said, he *knew* that. That same voice had come a little too late in telling him to shut his fucking trap.

Trixie, who he privately thought of as flaky, had at least been smart enough not to demand too much of him, and when he'd finally said he had enough, she'd nodded and moved on to the small black-haired woman in desperate need of some sun. Lying out by the beach, gazing up at the clear night sky, had been relaxing if a bit perplexing. It might be time for him to study the sky charts, because the stars seemed out of place tonight. But he had learned his lesson, and he wasn't about to tell anyone else his suspicions. If seeing a mermaid got him sent here, where the hell would telling someone the stars weren't in the right place land him?

A straitjacket, that's where.

Trixie signed his card, stating he had fulfilled his class. *Yep, that's nice, like being on probation.* No one else had to have their card signed. To his left, Rekkus and Cyrus came his way, standing to the side until he passed. They nodded at him before approaching Trixie. The secrecy on this island rivaled that of the CIA.

Picking up his sweatshirt, Kaleb yanked it on over his head, lowered the hood, and moved toward the main Haus. He hoped Serena would be waiting. She had said she would, but he couldn't read her. She went from being a full-out seductress to a giddy schoolgirl at hyper speed. When speaking to Rekkus, Cyrus, or any of the other men on the island, she came off as flirty and almost standoffish, but when she spoke to him, she seemed different. She flirted— he figured it was her second nature—but tinged with uncertainty that made him want to get to know the woman underneath.

Somehow, he knew there had to be more to her

than the sexy Siren she portrayed.

Striding up the candlelit gravel walkway, Kaleb stopped in his tracks to watch Serena through the open door. Seated behind the counter, on the computer…. He couldn't see her face, but her profile showed her intent on whatever she watched. She turned to the receptionist, who came to stand beside her and peered at the screen then typed something before going away again, leaving Serena to stare in rapture at the computer. Her expression reminded him of his four-year-old niece watching her cartoons. As if sensing him staring at her, she turned her head, and her face lit up, as if she had been counting the minutes until they were together again, and, somewhere in his gut, he hoped that had been the case, that this woman truly had been waiting for him.

Never taking his eyes off Serena, he strode with methodical steps into the soft light of the building. Kaleb watched her every move as she stood and walked around the reception desk with the grace of a ballerina. Even her dress, which covered very little, seemed to move with her as if it were alive. He so wanted to cup her face and bring his lips to hers that the need to do so caught him off guard.

"Hi." Her breathless voice washed over him like a warm breeze.

"Hi, yourself." He offered her his arm. "Shall we?"

"Okay." She placed her fingers in the crook of his arm.

"Do you need to get some shoes?" He pointed at her bare feet.

She shook her head. "I hate shoes."

"Stay away from the lake." Myron's voice drifted through the open doors.

"I heard you the first time, Myron."

"Why are we staying away from the lake?" he asked as they walked along the path away from the building.

"I have no idea, but when Myron's cards tell her something, you do it."

"Her cards? You mean the solitaire game she keeps playing?"

"She isn't playing a game. She's reading people."

"Like a fortune teller?"

Serena thought for a second then nodded.
"Something like that. More of a *future* teller."

"Right." Okay, so Serena might be as crazy as he
was. A thought both reassuring and a bit
disconcerting. Maybe this place, with its high-tech
security, might be a loony bin in disguise. And when
he'd come ashore, he'd been admitted and could
never leave. Serena said she had been here five
times—maybe she never left. If it was an asylum, that
would explain the tight security, and perhaps the
woman he had saved had been a suicide attempt. That
concept made a hell of lot more sense than a strange
current which shouldn't have found its way into a
lagoon, and this much security could be to restrain the
guests.

He'd been admitted to a high-class nuthouse.

"What are you thinking?"

"Oh, just figuring it all out in my head."

"What?"

He stopped walking and turned to face her, the
half-moon illuminating her face. "Let me ask you,

why are you here?"

"Oh, that would depend on whose side you were listening to."

"Your side."

"I'm here to try to figure out how not to be like my mother."

Kaleb wondered how bad a mother had to be that someone would seek help in the avoidance of becoming them. "Is she that bad?"

"She's a man-hating, murdering monster."

The anger and spite spewing from those supple lips shocked him, leaving no doubt in his mind Serena meant what she said. "Your mother is a murderer?"

"You know what? I've never said that aloud, but yes, and I hate her. I really, really hate her. I hate what she is, and what she does, and how she lures men into the deep with a seductive song and takes their final breath. I hate *her*." Taking a deep breath, she reached for the sky, stretching. "Wow, that felt good!"

"I can imagine."

"I don't know why I haven't said that sooner."

She focused on him. "What about you? Why are you here? And don't tell me because of your boss."

"I'm here because they all think I'm crazy." He kicked a stump with his heel because, after today's events, he'd begun to question his sanity.

She cocked her head. "Are you?"

"No, or at least I didn't think so, but being at this place makes me question what I thought I knew."

"Why do they think you're crazy?"

"You wouldn't believe me if I told you."

"Try me. I just told you my deepest harbored hatred of my mother. The least you can do is share your deep-seated crazy with me," she teased.

They had come to the cliffs over the ocean. The moonlight lit a runway across the rippling waters below. He couldn't face her, didn't want to see her laugh—or worse, agree he was crazy. "I tried rescuing a friend from the waters off the coast of Alaska. That area isn't kind on the best of days, and this was a Poseidon-releasing-his-wrath kind of day. A fishing vessel made a distress call. The ship had taken on water, and they had abandoned ship as it sank. I had already been in the water, getting a few men out of a raft. But we had a man in a survival suit still in the water. He'd been out there for an hour and didn't have much time, so my buddy Jim jumped in to help. I don't know what happened. He gave the thumbs up, and the mechanic brought up the rigging. But Jim wasn't with it. We lowered the wire to bring Jim up. Just then, a huge wave lifted the water within feet of the helo Jim reached out to grab hold, and a woman swam up beside him…and then he slipped under the water, staring up at me for a second before I lost him completely."

Serena laughed. "That's ridiculous."

Kaleb gritted his teeth so hard he might've crack one.

"Mermaids don't live in Alaska. It's too cold."

"Excuse me?" His breath escaped on a gasp.

"Why would any mermaid want to live in those waters? It's cold enough here."

Kaleb shook his head to clear it and turned to look at her. No one in all the times he'd told the story had reacted like she had. "Let me get this straight.

You aren't arguing with me that mermaids exist…only that they don't live in the Bering Sea?"

"Well, I suppose they could live there, but I can't imagine wanting to. I mean there—" She stopped, her mouth forming an O.

"You were saying?"

"Nothing." She fiddled with her skirt. "I don't think you're any crazier than anyone else here on the island."

He laughed. "You're not very reassuring."

"Was I supposed to say something else? What did you want me to say?"

This time, he did cup her cheeks, running his thumbs along the jawline, feeling the silky softness of her skin. "You said exactly the right thing."

"I did? Because with you, I feel like I'm always biting my tongue."

"Tripping over your tongue."

"See? Biting, tripping. I can't form a complete sentence around you."

"Talking is overrated." Brushing his lips against hers, Kaleb closed his eyes as Serena's breath rushed over him, warm and sweet. He deepened the kiss, taking advantage of the chance to taste this woman. His skin heated as soft, skilled fingers ran up his arms, over his shoulders, until long fingers laced into his hair. And just as he thought he was in control of the kiss, she took over, stepping closer into him, pressing her body against his. Touching him right where he needed her to, pressing when he needed it, and pulling away when he felt like he reached perfection.

She traced a line from his mouth to the erogenous zone behind his ear. "Take me back to your room," she whispered, nipping his earlobe ever so slightly.

His cock jumped to life, hard and hot. Damn, she might make him come right in his pants, and she'd only touched the skin around his face and neck. If he didn't do something, and quick, he'd embarrass himself. Why would this woman come back for seconds if he didn't have the control of a randy schoolboy getting his first blowjob? Shit, she hadn't even touched his cock.

Grabbing her wrist, he stepped away. "Let's take

a swim."

Cold Maine water would be perfect. But the thought of her swimming naked didn't cool his ardor one bit. The sudden need to swim with her overwhelmed his senses. Images of the water splashing over her naked body as he made love to her while the ocean surrounded them flooded his mind, spurring his need.

"No." Barely a whisper, but enough to stop him at the top of the path down to the beach. "No, I can't."

"Why not?" She'd been naked this afternoon, and she'd just suggested in the sexiest voice he'd ever heard they go back to his room. Why would she get shy now? "I'll even be a gentleman and turn my back until you're in the water."

"Please don't ask me why. I just can't." With that, she ran, ran from him, ran in the opposite direction—leaving him harder and hornier than he had ever been.

Kicking a stone on the path back to the Haus, Kaleb wondered if the water would be cold enough to ease the ache in him. Even a dip in the Bering Sea might not be cold enough tonight. "Yep, this is a fucking looney tunes island. *Crazy Haus* makes more sense."

Chapter Four

Cemil let the sand squish between his toes but stayed silent. Serena bit her bottom lip, certain the siblings would say they'd had enough of her antics and she needed to leave. But, this time, she really had tried to do the right thing. She had run as fast as she could, as long as she could, away from the temptation to take Kaleb up on his offer to swim.

Serena, having decided Cemil's silence had to be the nail in her locker, stood and walked toward the ocean. She took in the view one more time, hoping to catch sight of Kaleb if only once, to see him and hold that image in her head for eternity. As her toes hit the water, the familiar buzz of the ocean beckoned her home and welcomed her.

"Serena, where are you going?" Cemil glanced up from the patterns he had been drawing in the sand. "You always think the worst. Even when you've done nothing wrong."

"I seduced a man."

"Was he willing?"

"Yes." She nodded, but then they were all willing to an extent, weren't they? That's what made human men easy prey.

"Who initiated the kiss?"

"He did."

"Did you sing to him?"

Serena stepped back onto shore. "You know I can't sing. Rekkus has made sure of that."

"Did you hum?" Cemil peered at her knowingly.

"No." She supposed she shouldn't be surprised the witches knew her tricks. "I didn't try anything. It just happened, and then he asked me to swim."

"Swim? In these waters? Serena, there might be other reasons why a man chooses cold water over a warm bed." He sighed. "You have always stayed away from human men. You told us you never felt drawn to them. Perhaps you never felt you could trust yourself. You've only ever had sex with paras. Men who were never in danger of losing their hearts because, so far, no Fate has mated a mermaid to anyone since the last merman disappeared."

"I don't think I understand."

"Rekkus knew what you were. You came to him for sex—no more, no less. There was never a chance for there to be more. With Kaleb, there *is* something more. We all see it. Hell, Myron's cards feel it. It's stronger than what any of us can understand. It's called free will. Kaleb has it—every human does. It's his choice to come to you, to be with you. Paras find their mates, and the feelings come with that. Yes, that can be nice, but with Kaleb, he'll either choose you or not. He can choose to stay or walk away. And nothing you do or say will change the growing feeling he has for you."

"So I should leave."

"Why would you leave?"

Did she really have to confess all her failures to him? Wasn't this bad enough? "I can't give him children, can't swim with him, ever, and I can't be his mate."

"Wife. Humans don't have mates. Besides, I doubt he's thought that far ahead yet. I think his thoughts are more basic than that."

"So I should stay?"

"I would say you should." Cemil stood and let the wind blow through his long blond hair. "Besides, we have a favor to ask of you."

"Me?" Serena followed Cemil's gaze up the path from her cottage. Sarka, the only woman to make her mother come across like a cuttlefish, approached down the path. With her, a female shifter Serena had seen in the dining hall. The beautiful shifter, with sharp, exotic features. She stood a good five inches taller than Serena, with a svelte build. Long dark hair hung to her waist, and eyes the color of seaweed pierced Serena. Yet, with all her strength and beauty, nothing could hide the depth of her despair, and Serena sensed this woman had been beaten down until she couldn't fight anymore. Her left arm had been severed at the shoulder, and that said enough; shifters rarely were unable to heal on their own. Usually, if one lost a limb, it would repair itself while the shifter rested. But it required a deep rest, one where they'd have to rely on others to protect them from enemies.

Sarka stood before them. "Has she agreed, Cemil?"

"Hadn't gotten that far yet, but she will once she decides to stay."

"Your faith in her is far stronger than mine." Sarka turned to Serena. "Why the hell are you leaving now?"

"I can't stay. It could put the human at danger."

"Have him wear a condom. If you can't get pregnant, you can't kill him for his soul."

"Condom?" She pivoted so she could question Sarka and Cemil, clueless as to what this item might be.

"I am not having this conversation. I'll have a box delivered to your cabin. Believe me, he'll know what to do with them."

"But what if he doesn't?"

Cemil snickered, making Serena even more confused by the second.

Sarka scowled at Cemil then at Serena. "If he doesn't, you have my permission to take him out to sea and have your way with him. Because he would be too stupid to breathe."

"Sarka," Cemil bit out.

"What? Now." Sarka yanked the injured shifter forward none too gently. "Yavonka, this is Serena, our resident mermaid."

"No." Yavonka eyes went wide as she shook her head and walked away from the water's edge.

Serena closed her eyes, stepping into the water, letting it tell her what the shifter couldn't, or wouldn't. It would have been better had they both been in the water, but Serena's powers were stronger than most and she simply needed Yavonka near. The were-shark, scared and unable to shift safely because of the lost fin, fidgeted less, at ease in the presence of a mermaid. Not that Serena needed any powers to know that. With simple knowledge of a shark and their fins, she could deduce that simple enough. And everyone knew were-sharks were no great fans of merfolk. "Your school did this to you?"

"I will not get into that water with a Siren."

Serena opened her mouth and let out a high-pitch set of beeps and squeaks causing the were to cover her ears. "Get in the water, you useless fish."

Sarka's eyebrows shot up to her hairline. "Nicely played."

"Want to join her?" Serena asked.

"I'm a bitch, but that doesn't make me stupid." Sarka turned and dismissed the group with a haughty wave.

Yavonka slowly entered the water. Serena caught her breath at the despair and fear that came from the shark in painful waves. "Come on. You're safe in the harbor. I sense none of your school nearby." As she moved into the water, her dress floated on the surface until it became one with the ocean. Finally waist-deep, she dove in and swam deeper. Serena's legs fused into one, scales covering her lower body, starting at the waist and traveling down until it ended in a large fin. She paused for a moment as she forced her sonar through the protective walls of the island.

A few whales lingered beyond the island, and she smiled and sent out a greeting to the two old beings. Turning, she sensed Kaleb swimming in the harbor around the cliff. How she longed to swim to him, to feel his arms around her.

Then Yavonka entered the water, and Serena focused on the woman before her. She was scared to shift, scared she would go belly up and drown. Serena had to proceed with care. Swimming beside her, Serena sent out a call, urging the woman to shift. It took two more calls for the shark to do so, and then Yavonka's long hair wrapped around her like a blanket until the woman disappeared in the circle of black, emerging as the great beast of the sea. Yavonka's pointy nose and sharp teeth came straight at Serena's tail. But, a few feet from her, the shark lost her balance and flipped. Yavonka panicked, and Serena couldn't get hold of the shark to bring her to the surface. Forcing the shift from were into human, Yavonka struggled, frantic to get air as Serena fought her to get control. Eventually, she stopped playing nice and grabbed the woman by her good arm and yanked, pulling her upward. Yavonka was deeper than the human side of her could survive. The water in her lungs would kill her if Serena didn't push it out quickly. The curse of sea-animal weres—the water could kill them as quickly as the air.

Serena grabbed the other woman around the waist and forced her head and shoulders above the water. Yavonka sucked in air, gasping and coughing.

"Catch your breath, shark, then we'll try it again, but not so deep. If need be, I'll keep you upright while you rest."

"Why would you help me?"

"Why would I not?"

"Everyone in the ocean knows your mother. Why would any sea creature trust you?"

Serena focused on the horizon. "I am not my mother, just like you are not the killer your school wanted you to become. What happened to you?"

"My mate had his pet bull sharks attack me."

Turning her attention back to the other woman, she asked, "Why would he do that?"

Yavonka gazed out into the ocean toward the fog wall. "The betas in the school were getting restless. To prove no one was beyond his grasp and to show that he would attack anyone, he attacked me."

Serena had heard stories of were-sharks using

natural sharks to guard the schools while they slept, making already-aggressive animals into terrors of the sea. "Did he mean to kill you or only wound you?"

"I didn't stick around long enough to find out."

"We are a lot alike, me and you."

Yavonka nodded in reluctance before trying to shift again. Yavonka's inherent distrust of mermaids grew stronger in her animal form. It took four more tries before they figured out how to make it work. But, with each shift, the amount of time it took her animal side to calm down shortened, until the shark relaxed and fell into a trance-like sleep. Serena kept hold of the uninjured fin, allowing Yavonka to sleep without fear of tipping over. In the end, the only trick seemed to be that Serena needed to pet the shark before she fell asleep; otherwise, when she touched her, the beast would attack.

Swimming in a large circle as Yavonka entered the deep healing sleep, Serena let her gaze fall back to the shore. Cemil left her to her own devices. For the first time in a long time, she felt like she had a purpose. And by Poseidon, it felt good.

***

Kaleb hoped the laps would help. He'd blown off this morning's session of finding inner peace with the island's shaman. At this point, he didn't care if he never made it back to Alaska or his chopper with the others on his team. If he could just find relief from that damned woman, he'd be happy. Serena hadn't shown up for breakfast. He'd even come early and stayed until the last of the food had been taken away. She confused him and took up every waking moment of his thoughts. But when he closed his eyes, he had vivid dreams that had him waking up in a sweat, his cock aching for release.

When he'd asked Myron, she'd said Serena had a session with the siblings. Well, he had seen three of the siblings this morning already. The only one he hadn't seen had been the pale-blond brother. But he couldn't get any more information out of the receptionist to determine where he might find them. He didn't know where she stayed. If she was in the hotel, he hadn't found her room, and he'd knocked on every door on his floor. He knew there were cottages, but they were all over the island—some by the shore, others in the orchard, and a few hidden from prying eyes. Just his luck, she would be in the third.

Frustrated and exhausted from a night of restless sleep, Kaleb did what any rescue swimmer did to release tension—he swam. He stroked until his arms hurt and his legs throbbed, and then he pressed himself some more. Coming around the cliffs, to the harbor where he'd found the suicidal woman the day before, he stopped to tread water. When he saw Serena, swimming in the distance carefree, it sucker-punched him even this far away. He'd taken two strokes toward her when he saw the telltale signs of a fin breaking the water right behind her. *Shark.* He raced toward her with no thought or care for himself. The idea that she might be hurt made him swim harder than he ever had. Serena saw him then, an appearance of shock and panic overtaking her.

"Get out of the water! Shark!" he yelled.

She turned from him, and another woman

appeared next to her. Damn it, why were they still treading water and not moving? But, as he got closer, he saw they were moving to the shore, although slowly.

"Can you help Yavonka in?" she asked.

Serena seemed desperate to keep her distance from him.

"There's a shark!" He searched the area, trying to see if he could see it coming.

Serena smiled. "I know, but it won't bite. Not all sharks are man-eaters."

She was as crazy as they all thought he was. Arriving beside the woman in need of help, he noticed two things very quickly. A, she had a missing arm; and B, she swam nude. And if history was going to repeat itself, which it seemed to be doing, Serena would be naked as well. He would have closed his eyes, but his concern for the shark still in the area outweighed any need to be a gentleman. He swam next to the other woman, who moved with a strong modified sidestroke. As they neared the shore, both women stopped. Kaleb paused to tread water.

"Yavonka is naked. Could you close your eyes so she can get out of the water?" A tone of impatience he wouldn't have associated with Serena edged her voice. He turned his back on the two and did as he was told, closing his eyes and waiting for the first set of feet splashing through the shallow water, followed by the second. He heard Serena say they would continue to work tomorrow and Yavonka thank her.

"She's gone. You can open your eyes now." Kaleb turned around and found Serena standing naked on the beach, skin glistening in the sun as she headed for one of two cottages on the shore. He watched Serena's hips move as she walked away. He marveled that her hair seemed almost dry as she moved onto the porch.

She opened the door, turning to throw over her shoulder, "Are you going to stare, or are you coming in?"

Come in? Oh, he hoped so. Jogging up, Kaleb stopped before the door. "Do you have a towel? My trunks are dripping, and I don't want to leave puddles on your floor."

"Just take them off. You won't need them." Serena ran her fingers between his cool skin and the waistband. "You'll certainly be more comfortable without."

"Is that so?" He swallowed.

"Definitely so." She yanked the cotton cord, untying it. Ever so slowly, Serena worked the wet fabric over Kaleb's hips; every muscle in his body clenched in anticipation. He was wound tighter than a watch spring and wasn't going to do anything to make her run tonight. But if she didn't relieve this ache within him, nothing would.

"About last night on the cliffs…."

"We can talk later, if you're still up to it."

She moved to her knees, working his trunks down legs that seemed to refuse to let it go. They clung like a person fighting to stay in a boat sinking into the ocean. A quick, strong tug and the suit landed with a sloppy thud at his feet. He picked up one foot at a time, stepping out of the suit. As if she could sense what he wanted, she removed the offending fabric, before peering up at him from her submissive position.

Serena's bright, wide eyes were a color he had never seen on a person before. The hue of the bluest ocean, and they seemed to churn within their depths, blues swirling into one another. And her mouth held the natural red of the sunrise over the Bering Sea. How he longed to feel that mouth over his cock and balls. As he envisioned it, she did exactly that. She took his protruding cock into her warm, wet mouth, licking and sucking from the head all the way down and then up again. With her tongue, she worked her way down to his balls, licking them then taking each one into her mouth one at a time.

She kneaded his balls as she took him deep into her mouth again. Closing his eyes, Kaleb fisted Serena's hair, helping her find the rhythm he liked. She seemed to know what he wanted a second before he did. Her mouth worked him until he thought he would explode, but he wanted to be in her. He wanted them both together, not just her on her knees, satisfying him.

"Condoms. Do you have any?"

"Um, yes. I think so." She searched around.

"You don't know?"

"Sarka said she would have Myron bring some to me."

"You talked to Sarka about getting you some condoms?"

"Actually, she suggested it."

"Who else knows you were planning to bring me here to seduce me?"

Serena cocked her head for a second and shrugged. "Most everyone, I would guess."

Most everyone. It wasn't that he cared, but, as a private person, having his business known by so many disturbed him. His crew never knew when he dated anyone, and he never kissed and told. Finding the object of his interest in the corner, he went to the side table and picked up a full box of XL condoms. With a note on top.

Kaleb, Hope they fit. Have fun, Myron.

Serena looked at the box and then back to him. He had a sinking suspicion she had no idea what they were or how they were used. "Have you ever used a condom before?"

She shook her head. "There has never been the need before."

Perhaps she'd been on the pill in the past. But Kaleb had filled out a full health report, and she must have done the same over the last five times she'd been here. The staff wouldn't encourage her to have sex with someone if she had a sexually transmitted disease.

So she didn't know how to use a condom. He did, and it could be just as much fun teaching her how to put them on him. But not this time. He lacked the stamina or willpower to last through that kind of lesson.

He opened the package and rolled the latex over his cock. Her head tilted to the side as she observed his covered cock. "I have so much to teach you, don't I?"

Her gaze lifted again to his face, and the seductress returned, her pink tongue escaping her lips long enough to wet them and drive him wild. "Let me do the teaching tonight." Serena's voice came out on a husky breath.

She placed a warm palm on his chest just over his heart. She had the power to make it stop. His breath caught, and, for a moment, their eyes met. He could find no sign of the insecure woman from dinner and their walk the night before. This sex goddess had him in her sights. Pushing gently, she backed him up until the back of his knees hit the chair in the corner.

"Sit," she murmured, throwing her hair over her shoulder before straddling his hips. "There may be a lot of things I have left to learn, but seducing you is something I know I can excel at."

"I'm convinced you can." His head fell back as she explored his chest. Fingers traced every muscle from his collarbone to his abs. Kaleb's muscles clenched as she reached between them and grabbed his hard cock and brought it to her opening. With slow, almost painful precision, she encased him in her warmth, holding him tight. Kaleb gritted his teeth, grasping onto her hips. Every ounce of testosterone in him demanded he enter her, take her as his.

He had never felt a need this intense for anyone

in his entire life. Her eyes were closed as she moved in a slow, dance-like rhythm. Her thighs tightened against his every time she moved up over his cock. As she slowly descended again, her full breasts, inches from his mouth, were a temptation he couldn't resist. Wrapping an arm around her waist, Kaleb eased her toward him, taking one full nipple into his mouth while his free hand palmed and kneaded the other.

Serena's breath caught, renewing his determination to show her what he could give her. Her pace picked up, her vaginal walls tightening around him, squeezing him until Kaleb nearly couldn't control his orgasm. With every bit of discipline he had, he staved off the finish, this need to pump his seed deep into her. God, he had never wanted to have unprotected sex until right now, and every bit of him screamed to remove the condom. Primal needs he didn't think he could command demanded he give her what she needed to create new life.

He moved his touch down to her hips again, to

slow her down, to take back control. His fingers bit into her round ass cheeks as he forced her down, hoping to make her pause for a second. Instead, he entered her until he could go no farther, and she shattered above him, her head thrown back.

Kaleb had a perfect view of Serena's graceful throat as she fought for air. Her hair tickled his knees, but the only thing he could focus on was her body shaking over him. A sound, not quite a song, but not a scream, came from her mouth. It hit him square in the heart and filled his whole body with a warmth that could become addicting.

"You are so beautiful."

"Kaleb, help me," she whispered, moving on him faster.

He wrapped one arm around her waist and looped the other behind her and rested on her shoulder. He urged her closer and forced her to take every inch of him. She bucked as he pressed his hips up. And then she fell apart in his arms again, a second orgasm overcoming her. She collapsed into him, kissing his shoulder as he continued his assault on her body. Over and over, he fucked her until his own overwhelming needs returned. Standing up, he positioned her legs around his waist and walked the few feet toward the bed. Lowering both of them, he ran fingers through her hair, drinking in every inch of her face before taking her lips in an all-consuming kiss.

With the bed as leverage, he drove into her. She tightened her legs around his waist, raking her nails down his back. She arched away from him, panting again. Too lost in his own desire to focus on her making that amazing sound, all he wanted was to feel her fracture below him at the same time he did. Just as he didn't think he would be able to hold off any longer, she arched her back off the bed and yelled his name.

And the world went black as he came harder than he ever had in his life. The air left his lungs, and his heart slowed. Kaleb's last thought before he collapsed on top of her, if this was how he died, then what a way to do it.

Panicked, Serena felt his body twitch and then fall still. His breathing stopped. Shaking him, she didn't know what to do. They weren't in the water, and the condom prevented his seed from getting to her. Oh, she felt the draw to have it. She craved to feel it inside her, reaching into her womb.

"No!" she screamed, lifting his head and placing her lips against his. Then, ever so slowly, she brushed them. "No, Kaleb. Please, no."

A single tear escaped her eye. Shocked, she reached up to touch it. She had never cried before, and as the tear crystallized into stone on her finger, it changed to a vibrant orange, the color of the sunset on the horizon. She turned her head to find his palm up and open. Placing the sea glass into his palm, she whispered, "I give you my tears, Kaleb. Breathe for me. Take my breath."

Nothing. He didn't move, and Serena's despair deepened as she closed his fingers around the item and tightened her grip on him. She had failed at everything—the condom hadn't saved him from her. And now, she didn't even have his baby. Gulping air to fill lungs compressed by his weight, Serena shoved at his body.

Then his eyes fluttered open, and a smile came to his lips as he took a deep, life-sustaining breath. Reaching up, Serena kissed him hard, putting all her relief into it. *Good God. That was close. Too close.*

Lifting up, he smiled. "You are amazing."

"So are you."

"We need to talk," Kaleb said, rolling away, but bringing her with him as he went.

Amazed by the sense of closeness, Serena nuzzled against his shoulder. His scent overwhelmed her until she couldn't help but lick and kiss the side of his neck. Relief washed over her. She hadn't killed him. Or at least could turn it around if she had.

"I can think of better things to do than talk," she murmured against his ear.

"You'll have to give me a few minutes to recover. I'm only human, you know. I've never blacked out like that before. What are you trying to do, kill me?"

Serena eased away from him, backing off the

bed. "Why would you say that?"

"What are you talking about?"

"Why would you say I was trying to kill you? I would never hurt you. You have to believe me."

Raising himself up onto his elbows, Kaleb stared at her. "Serena, it was a joke."

"It wasn't funny."

Sighing, he fell back onto the pillow and rubbed his face. He lay so still, she worried he wouldn't say anything at all. Then he turned his head toward her and gave her a smile that made her knees tremble. "You're right. With your mother and your history, that wasn't funny. I didn't think. I'm sorry."

She placed her fingers in his rough palm, letting him bring her back into the bed and into his arms. Only then did he notice the stone in his other hand.

"What is this?"

"A piece of sea glass I found today. I thought of you. I wanted to give it to you as a gift." Not a lie, not really.

"Wow, it's in the shape of a tear. You know what they call sea glass?"

She shook her head, watching him hold the stone to the light.

"Sailors say sea glass is the tears of a mermaid."

"Do they?"

"I love it. Thank you." He palmed it again, smiling up at her.

"You're welcome."

"Now, I need a shower. Would you like to join me? Or we could swim."

"No swimming."

"So I am coming to understand." He threw his legs over the side of the bed, turning his back to her. "Perhaps, one day, you will tell me why you have no issues fucking my brains out but a simple swim is out of the question."

"It's safer that way, but a shower sounds nice." Well, a shower *sounded* nice, not that she had ever taken one.

"What I'm thinking is nothing nice at all." Locking his lips with hers he walked them both into the bathroom. He stepped away long enough to remove the used condom before turning on the shower. "I hope Myron has more than one box of condoms on this island."

"She originally gave me one condom then decided a box would be better."

"I think I need to get Myron a present."

"What kind of present?"

"I'm sure we can think of something. I guess that will depend on how many we use. Do you think anyone is going to come hunting for me if we don't make it to dinner?"

"Dinner? *Oh no.*" The siblings were going to kill her. She knew better than to break any more rules.

At that moment, a knock on the door echoed through the cabin. "I am guessing that's a yes."

Serena made a move to the door and giggled when Kaleb handed her a robe. Humans and their need to be covered up. Like any para would care what she went to the door in. He stood next to her as she opened the door to find Cyrus standing there, glowering.

"You need to get to the dining hall for dinner. I am not a goddamned babysitter."

"We know. We lost track of time." Serena did her best to appear contrite.

"Let me get dressed, and I'll come right up."

As Kaleb picked up his swimsuit and walked into the other room, Cyrus whispered, "I need the tear."

"What?"

"Myron is in a fit. Her cards said Kaleb died. We were about to raise almighty hell when Myron said you had saved him with a tear. I need that tear. Sarka needs to place it in a necklace for him to wear."

"Will that protect him?"

"If you don't have any intercourse with him unless he wears a condom until he can wear that tear over his heart."

"Okay." Running into the other room, she pried the piece of glass out of Kaleb's fist. "Trust me," she said, kissing his lips before taking the tear to Cyrus, who promised to have it back to them in the morning.

Passing Serena an ornate wooden box, he paused for a second before turning to leave. "This is for you, and you have ten minutes to get your asses in the dining room because next it will be Rekkus pounding your door off its hinges."

Serena closed the door behind her and moved into the kitchen area where Kaleb stood in his damp swim trunks. She gave him the wooden box. He let out a laugh when he lifted the top. Before Serena could ask, he held up a stash of condoms in a variety of colors.

"Do we need another box?" she asked.

"They seem to have a great deal more confidence in my stamina than I do."

Serena licked her lips just thinking about the ways they could use those condoms.

"Whatever you're thinking, stop. If we don't show up for dinner, one of those security goons will break your door down."

"You're no fun." She pouted.

"Is that so? I'll show you after dinner exactly how fun I can be. Now, go and change."

From somewhere outside the cabin, Cyrus yelled, "Five minutes!"

Chapter Five

Kaleb sat on a natural underwater stone bench that ran along the inner rim of the hot springs, Serena straddling him. The sun's rays played over the water as the sun made its final descent into the west. Kaleb's fingers went to his new necklace and the sea glass attached to it. Sarka's thank you for saving the swimmer caught in the riptide. Kaleb had only taken it off once since, and even then he'd found he didn't want it gone. Strange, the need to touch a piece of glass. When he couldn't touch it, Kaleb felt empty somehow.

The past several days had gone at a far different pace than the first couple. He no longer took classes on *breathing* and *finding your center*. His new sessions were physically draining and seemed more like training than healing. Was there something healing about getting your ass kicked by the security guard from hell? But, Kaleb had to admit, after each session, he did feel stronger and more centered.

His meals had changed, too. No longer did he have to suffer grubs and greens—instead, they served him protein and carbs. He had free time in the afternoon to swim but did his best to stay away from where Serena worked with Yavonka. Serena seemed more at peace, as well. Perhaps because they no longer fought their needs for each other, the stress lessened, or maybe she just enjoyed helping the young woman with the missing arm learn to swim again.

But when Cyrus suggested he stay on another week for more healing, Kaleb had hesitated. He'd felt ready to head back and hoped he could pass his psych eval this time so he could return to work. Only when Cemil mentioned that Serena had agreed to extend her stay to help Yavonka did Kaleb agreed to remain, on the one condition he move into Serena's cabin. He hadn't actually spent another night in his room since they finally made love. After a few whispers between the three present siblings and a growl from Rekkus, they agreed.

So, the next week began much as the last had

ended. He woke early to make love to Serena and then had a quick breakfast in the dining hall. Serena would go off to do whatever she did when not working with Yavonka. He would head off to tai chi with Cemil, followed by a strange form of aikido with Rekkus—also known as *getting your ass kicked by a big thug with attitude*—then lunch, where he ate alone. His afternoon started with a quick swim, a massage with Lakshmi, and then back to getting his ass kicked by Rekkus. If Rekkus was unavailable for the ass-kicking, Cyrus seemed more than willing to take over. But Kaleb's evenings left him free, free to walk the island with Serena.

Their favorite place to go, the hot springs, lay off the beaten track. His achy muscles never seemed to hurt much after sitting in the hot water, and although she wouldn't swim with him in the ocean and certainly not in the lake—they had been warned *ad nauseum* to stay away—she had no issues making love to him and draining the rest of his energy at the springs.

Serena laid her head against his shoulder. "I

don't think I can walk home."

Home. He loved the sound of that but wondered what would happen when he left in four days. He feared he might be falling in love for the first time in his life, but Serena planned to stay for a while to come, and though he could justify one more week, his time to leave loomed. "I can carry you."

"What? Have I left you with so much energy you can hike with not just your weight but mine as well?" Still straddling him, she lifted up to see him better in the glowing moonlight, her fingers grazing his shoulder. "Your bruise is already fading."

Craning his neck to see, he nodded. All of his injuries healed much quicker on the island. "It will only be replaced by another tomorrow."

"Rekkus is a brute."

"He's a hard taskmaster. And I'm getting better already. By the end of the week, I might actually be able to take him down."

"Let me come see that." Serena smiled, her eyes twinkling.

He loved her like this, when she relaxed and left

herself unguarded. This moment always took place in water. On land, she tried too hard. Like she knew she didn't fit in. At first, he had chalked it up to her past relationship with Rekkus and the tension there. But both she and Rekkus acted exactly the same no matter who was present. With the exception of when Dana came around—then, Rekkus went from what he would call a wild animal to a pussycat in seconds.

Interesting, that. He supposed even the mighty fell sometimes.

But still the unanswered questions swirled in his brain about what the hell went on behind the scenes of this island. Kaleb had stumbled across a bizarre barracks-like building in the woods. Though empty, it stood ready for occupants—and soon. And what about the second dock on the other side of the island that he would have missed had he not stopped to retie his shoe. Only when he knelt did the camouflage around the dock seem odd enough to make him give it a another glance. Upon closer inspection, the small shed near the dock housed a state-of-the-art cigarette boat, capable of high speeds.

On top of everything else, he puzzled over the unexplained booms followed by earth tremors on Saturday morning, waking him from a deep sleep. He had jumped up and run to stand in the doorway, years of training come to life. Serena had refused to budge from the bed and mumbled something about it happening at sunup and sundown every Saturday then fell asleep again. Sure enough, the boom happened again at sunset, and he wondered how he had missed that the day he'd arrived.

But then he remembered he had been asleep, and Rekkus had said something about Sage "overdoing it." Were the Rowans drugging people? If so, why? They genuinely seemed to want to help those staying on their island. Well, the lighter two did. The darker two brooded, and Cyrus did seem to get great pleasure out of throwing Kaleb to the ground—by far his favorite move. Sarka ignored everyone unless forced to acknowledge them. And he'd only seen Sarka use the first elevator. Where did it go?

Soft lips against his pulse brought him back from his musing. "You're an insatiable minx."

"Only with you." Serena cradled his face. "I don't want you to leave on Saturday."

"I can't stay here. I need to get back to work, or at least try."

She sighed, the sound ripping at something inside of him. "I know but...."

"You could come to Alaska."

She lifted her head with a jolt. "You would want me to come to Alaska? To be with you?"

"I just asked you, didn't I?"

"Alaska is really cold."

"Is that a yes?"

She pulled away from him and floated to the center of the pool. "I want to say yes."

"Then say yes."

When Serena didn't answer, he moved toward her. He cupped her face, forcing her to meet his eyes. So many emotions swirled within their depths. A part of Kaleb thrilled that she would consider it, but the other part of him felt a bitter stab of disappointment that she hadn't jumped at the idea. He'd never asked a woman to live with him before, so to have her stumble over her answer hurt more than his pride.

"It's not that easy."

"Yesss." He drew out the word as long as he could. "Very easy."

She expelled one of those sighs women the world over made when they thought men didn't have a single brain cell between them. "I can't explain now, but I want to come. I really do. I'm not sure how we would make it work."

"We leave here on the boat that takes us back to the mainland. From there, we drive to Bangor and catch a flight to Alaska."

She gnawed her bottom lip and twisted away. Damn it, he wouldn't beg her to follow him. Lifting his arms from the water, he eased himself out to sit on the edge of the spring. When she didn't make any move to turn back toward him, Kaleb cursed, got to his feet, and walked over to the discrete towel rack a few feet away.

"Is the thought of living with me so troubling?"

"No! It's not that."

Wrapping the towel around his waist, he rounded

toward her. "Then what is it? Explain it to me."

"Alaska is really cold."

"Yes, it can be cold, but it's summer right now and the temperatures aren't much different there than they are here." When she didn't answer, he grabbed his pants, pulled them on, jammed his feet into his shoes, and started walking away. "You know what? If all you wanted was a holiday lay, then you should have said so."

Angry at her, disgusted with himself, and peeved with the damned Master Chief who had him sent here, Kaleb stormed down the moonlit path toward the cabin. He didn't want to go back there, not tonight, and he cursed giving up his room. Why the hell didn't this place have a bar or something? A fucking beer would do the trick right now.

God, how stupid could he be, thinking she would follow him to Alaska or that she could be interested in anything other than his cock?

"Mother fucker!"

"Excuse me?"

Dana? Coming out of the wooded area, basket

over her arm. "What are you doing in the woods at this time of night?"

"I wanted some apples." She smiled and offered him one.

Kaleb took it, not sure why, but took it nonetheless. "You couldn't have waited until morning? Where's Rekkus?"

"Why does everyone ask that? We aren't joined at the hip. And if I want an apple, I will get an apple." She stomped her foot and headed down the path.

Okay, crazy hormonal woman. "At least let me walk you back." He started after her.

"Suit yourself," she mumbled before stopping so fast Kaleb nearly bumped into her. "Sorry, I'm feeling a little smothered right now, and with the full moon coming, it's only going to get worse. Rekkus won't let me out at night in a few more days. You know I love the big lug, but he can be a bit on the high-and-mighty side."

"You don't say?" He wanted to say, *No kidding,* but felt it better to keep his opinions to himself. He grabbed the basket of apples from her for lack of something better to do.

"Where's Serena?"

"We aren't joined at the hip, you know."

Dana smiled, and her shoulders relaxed as she started walking again. "Sorry, really, but you two are never far from the other."

"Yes, well, that will change soon. I'm leaving on Saturday."

"And?"

"And I asked her to go with me, and in not so many words she let me know she wasn't interested."

"Oh. I see."

"I'm glad someone does."

"You're heading back to Alaska, yes?"

He nodded, an uncomfortable lump forming in his throat.

"You do realize that other than her family's hunting grounds and this island, she hasn't been anywhere else? I'm sure the thought of going so far away is terrifying for her. She's never flown, and she has to swim every day for her sanity. And, in her mind, Alaska's waters might be too cold."

"There are indoor pools."

"Right, but I doubt she knows about them." He would have questioned that crazy statement when Dana continued. "She's led a sheltered life."

"No one is that sheltered." He thought for a second then remembered their first conversation. "Okay, she has been sheltered."

They got to her cabin, and Dana turned, taking the basket back. "One day, I hope she'll open up to you. There is so much about her you don't know. But I think she loves you, and I don't think she's ever felt that before."

"Dana!" Rekkus growled. Kaleb had ceased wondering how he made those deep strange sounds, and had even caught himself trying to mimic them in the shower. "Where the hell were you? Cyrus and I have been searching the damned island—"

"You're smothering me, you damned cat." She stormed into the cabin, slamming the door.

"Smothering…what…grrrrr…*ffyc…mae hi wedi cachi arna I."* Rekkus sat in the chair on the porch— more like threw himself into it—and banged the back of his head against the cabin a few times for good measure.

Kaleb should have enjoyed his tormentor's discomfort, but it hit too close to home tonight.

Giving him an inch, Kaleb offered, "She was in the orchard. I ran into her on the path coming back."

"Apples. Again? I just got her damned apples this morning." Rekkus stood up and peeked in the window of the cabin. "She is going to make me crazy, that one."

Feeling it safer to keep his mouth shut, Kaleb applauded that he had at least learned that skill on his visit here. He stayed quiet as Rekkus lifted the walkie-talkie and responded to Cyrus's asking if anyone had found her. And, Kaleb supposed, had Serena gone for a walk in Alaska in the middle of the night, he, too, might have panicked.

"Thank you for seeing her home safe. I know it's stupid, but I hate not being able to protect her all the time, and, yes, I know she wants more space, damn it. Thanks again." Rekkus moved to the door, bracing himself before opening it. Kaleb had to give the man props for quick reflexes as he caught the three apples hurled at him in succession. "Stay single, Kaleb. It's so much safer," Rekkus muttered before shutting the door behind him.

"He needs to give her some breathing room," Serena said from behind Kaleb. "That's all she wants."

Filling his lungs with air until it hurt, he steeled himself before turning to face her. "I don't think it's in his nature."

"You could be right." She stepped toward him but paused, unsure again. "I'm sorry if I hurt your feelings earlier. It's not that I don't want to be with you it's just…."

"Alaska's cold?"

She nodded. "Really—"

Kaleb shushed her before moving her face to his so he could kiss her senseless. "We'll figure something out."

"Okay."

Kaleb smiled against her lips. "Okay."

Chapter Six

Swish—Rekkus's fist barely missed hitting the side of Kaleb's head. He might not be able to land many on the man, but at least Kaleb had gotten good at avoiding taking some on his own. But, today, Rekkus kept stopping to sniff the air—a strange thing for anyone to do, in Kaleb's honest opinion. All over the island, one could feel the sense something odd was in the air.

Everyone from Myron to Rekkus acted...off. Serena had been taken aback when Yavonka announced at breakfast she didn't want to swim today, saying she didn't feel safe. Serena had excused herself and gone to find Cyrus. When she returned, she said she needed to take a quick swim and would see him "after his ass whooping."

Even though her voice remained light, she appeared distracted. At first, he chalked it up to the tension still between them since their discussion at the hot springs, but he didn't think so. Not focused on the man before him, Kaleb hadn't braced himself for the kick to the chest that sent him flying. Expecting the usual reproof he received when Rekkus gained the advantage, Kaleb couldn't hide his surprise to be helped to his feet.

"I think we should call it a day."

"A day? You've made contact with me twice, hardly the *beat the shit out of the guest* you usually go for."

"It would appear neither of us is focused today."

"What the hell is going on?"

Rekkus seemed about to say something but shook his head. "I hope to be able to tell you very soon, but not yet. Do me a favor. Would you go check on Dana on your way back to your cabin?"

"Of course." The hairs on the back of Kaleb's neck stood on end, and, seconds later, the alarm on Rekkus's walkie-talkie went crazy. "But I think the soon just became now."

"Damn it. Come with me." Rekkus turned off the alarm and tore off as Cemil squawked at him to get his ass to the lake, immediately. "You, I think, are about to find out the island's little secret."

Rekkus ran through the woods with Kaleb fast on his heels, though it took every ounce of energy he had to keep up. When the woods opened to the forbidden lake, Kaleb stopped and leaned over his knees to catch his breath. Finally able to breathe, he stood. A small group of beautiful women stood waist-deep in the lake. And they were glaring.

Glaring at Serena, who gave back every ounce of anger they threw at her. In the face of the most imposing of the women, Kaleb saw what he couldn't believe he had missed at first glance. This had to be Serena's mother.

Kaleb walked closer and would have taken Serena in his arms, but Cemil placed a staying arm in his path. "I wouldn't, if I were you."

"I'm not afraid of a little cat fight."

"Cat fight doesn't begin to explain it. And here comes Sarka. This is gonna get ugly." Cyrus dug a set of orange earplugs out of his pocket and placed one in his ear.

"What are you doing?"

"Earplugs. Should have brought you a set, I guess." He shrugged as he shoved the second into his other ear.

"What the hell is going on?" Sarka demanded, stepping within inches of the lake.

"What?" Cyrus barked.

Cemil turned his attention to Sarka who stood next to Serena.

"You're not welcome here, Mother."

"Serena, your year is up," her mother said in a calm manner that belied the tension surrounding them.

"That's not possible."

"Your year is up as of sundown tonight."

Two of the women came forward, and, as Kaleb got ready to jump in, Sarka put herself between the women in the water and Serena. "I do believe Serena informed you that you aren't welcome here."

"I do not listen to you, witch."

"Oh, I think you'll be listening to me. This island isn't big enough for more than one bitch, and that bitch is me. Now, I suggest you remove yourselves from my island before I have my security team throw your scaly asses off."

Rekkus growled and stepped toward Serena, grabbed her by the arm, and hurled her into Kaleb's arms. "When your sisters start singing, you need to sing like your life depends on it."

"But—"

"Make that sing like *his* life depends on it, and you know it does."

Rekkus started to strip naked, leaving Kaleb gaping. "What's he going to do, fuck them off the island?"

Cyrus looked confused, pointing to his ear and shaking his head. "What did you say? What did he say?"

Then everything seemed to fall into place as one of the women dove into the water, her *tail* making a loud splash. Processing that information, Kaleb saw something even stranger if possible. A pale-green tinted white glow surrounded Sarka, spreading out to the people standing with her. Others, all women from the Haus, had joined the group: Myron, Trixie,

Lakshmi. He counted thirteen arrivals, not including Rekkus, Serena, and himself. And, somewhere in his subconscious, Kaleb knew Sarka had called in her coven.

"Siren, sing!" Rekkus demanded. And then he did the impossible. Where a naked Rekkus had once stood, a large, angry black tiger took his place. And the damned tiger seemed to shrug at him before leaping to the water's edge. No way had that just happened. Kaleb turned to Cemil for answers.

"You did call it a cat fight." Cemil shrugged before patting Serena on the shoulder. He dragged Cyrus away before the man could say *what* again.

Kaleb's head spun. Too much odd information came at him all at once. He turned to Serena, closed his eyes, and prayed that when he opened them, he would be in bed with her, and this weird dream would evaporate into that mystical arena all dreams went.

Instead, he found her watching him with a sad little smile. "If you believe nothing, believe I love you."

"Serena?"

"I am so sorry." Serena took him with her, until her feet touched the water then opened her lips. The most beautiful voice began to sing to him. One line, and everything around him faded to nothing.

"Keep singing," Cemil said from behind Serena.

Her mother and sisters all sang together, trying to drag the men with them into the depths of the lake, but they hadn't anticipated the Rowan siblings were well prepared for nearly any situation.

Her focus remained on Kaleb, the man she loved, the man who would never see her the same again. She sang like she had never sung before. And she knew she had him, knew she could, at that moment, drag him into the depths of the ocean, and he would put up no fight. He would die just to have her one more time. Her heart broke. Kaleb, the man whose only goal in life had been to rescue people, would awaken from her spell and wish her dead.

She could hear the frustration in her mother's voice as it turned from glowing beauty to shrieking disbelief. "What kind of magic is this?" she demanded with such rage even her sisters were forced to stop singing.

Serena stepped away from Kaleb. Her spell would last a few more minutes. "Mother, it's over. Leave, please."

"Why did our songs have no effect on the men?" her youngest sister demanded in a snit.

Cemil smiled. "Because, my dear, what you have to offer doesn't interested me in the least."

Her mother started out of the water but stopped as Rekkus reared back on his haunches and gave her a warning swipe.

"Be careful, sea witch. Our kitty here has a taste for fish." Sarka laughed.

"And him." She pointed to Cyrus. "How did our song not affect him?"

"Huh? What did she say? I can't hear a dammed thing," Cyrus yelled.

"You see, Mother? They were ready for you. Please leave. Let me be."

"But you are to be queen one day." Her mother's face softened.

Serena entered the water and grabbed her hand. "I can't be the mermaid you need me to be. I can't kill a man to create another life. I just can't be that creature."

Her mother sighed and nodded. "I would like to force it, but it appears I have been outmatched by a team of witches and a cat. You are my daughter and rightful heir to the throne. I can't change that, and neither can you. But perhaps Poseidon himself has a different path for you. It would be best if you didn't return to the palace for now. I shall send for you when the time is right."

Serafina hugged her sister. "I shall miss you."

They turned away and headed into the water, one by one disappearing into the depths of the lake.

"Call if you are ever in need. I will come," Serafina said before disappearing with a splash of her tail.

Serena walked to the starry-eyed Kaleb and placed a palm against his cheek. She brushed her lips against his and receded into the water. Her despair overcoming her, the shallow waters of the lake churned as if a hurricane had blown in.

"Where are you going?" Sage asked, walking ankle deep into the lake, water splashing at her skirt.

"It's time for me to leave."

"What?" Cyrus asked before Sarka smacked the back of his head. Smiling with a faint flush, he removed the earplugs. "How long will the spell last?"

"Not much longer now, I should think. But when he awakens, I cannot bear to see the hatred in his eyes."

"You can't know that," Sage offered, rubbing Serena's bare arm.

"I can." She glanced at Cemil, somewhat hopeful and praying that he would contradict her, but he shook his head. "Please, someone tell him I did...*do* love him. And always will."

Tears blurred her vision, making Serena unaware of Sarka standing before her until the woman lifted a handful of sea glass in an array of colors for her to see. "Perfect," Sarka murmured.

Sage, never one for anger, looked aghast. "Give those back."

"Why? She doesn't need them."

"She's right. I have no use for them at all. Keep them."

Serena turned and dove into the water, giving her friends one last wave with her tail before following her family through the caves that led from the lake to the ocean, propelling herself hard and fast, unsure where she would go. Unsure where she would be welcome.

Chapter Seven

Kaleb's head felt like it had been ripped in two, and he couldn't deal with what had just happened to his heart. The fog had yet to lift from the edges of his vision, making him feel as if he were walking in a dream. He needed off this island—now. He would head back to Alaska and pretend none of this had happened. He would lie his way through his psych evals and get right back in that chopper. And he would hunt down and kill whatever mermaid crossed his path.

Throwing his duffle bag over his shoulder, he stormed out of the cabin. Serena had not returned yet, but, then, he hadn't expected her to. Walking to the water's edge, he ripped the silver chain she had given him from his neck. The sea glass glimmered in the late afternoon light. He palmed it for a second. She had been good, he would give her that. Good at deception, good in bed, and good at making him appear and feel like an ass. Winding back, he let loose and threw the necklace as far as he could into the ocean.

"Take your fucking tears, Serena. I neither want nor need them!" he yelled into the cove. When the stone hit the water, he doubled over in agony, as if someone had punched him in the gut. And if he didn't already know he was crazy, Kaleb would have sworn he heard Serena cry out in the distance.

"Are you okay?"

Kaleb turned to see Dana a few feet from him, her expression of concern almost too much to bear. "I don't know," he finally said.

Dana took a tentative step toward him. She reached out to touch him, but refrained. "I do understand. I'm merely human, too. When I first saw Rekkus shift, I didn't handle it well."

Kaleb nodded and gave her what he hoped read as a kind smile. He readjusted his sack and started toward the Haus. *It isn't the same. How could it be?* He doubted Dana had watched her best friend be killed by a were-monster. He couldn't even begin to wrap his head around *that* piece of information.

The island lay eerily quiet, not even the birds chirping. As if everything held its breath. Somehow, he knew the day wasn't over, and it was going to get worse before he could get his ass back to the mainland.

When he entered the lobby, Myron met his gaze. "You're expected in the office."

"Did your damned cards tell you that?"

Myron smiled and shook her head. "No, Rekkus did."

Kaleb dumped his bag in the lobby, not caring where it landed, and walked around the desk to the office. He didn't even bother to knock, he was that done with the place.

When Kaleb went in, all conversation stopped. Five sets of eyes focused on him, but no one said anything. Not that he expected they would.

"I want off the island now, tonight. And don't give me shit about the boat coming once a week because I've seen the other dock."

Sarka raised her eyebrows and stood. "I think I'll let you men deal with this." She left, followed by

Sage, who smiled.

"And when speaking of men, she means these two. Should you need me, just yell," Cemil said to no one in particular and closed the door on his way out.

"Well?"

"Have a seat." Cyrus indicated the seat Sage had vacated.

"I prefer to stand."

"Suit yourself." Rekkus drew a thick file out of a drawer and slammed it on the desk. "We've been watching you for years now."

"What the fuck?" Leaning over, Kaleb grabbed the thick folder. The dossier started with a photo of him from high school.

Cyrus again indicated the empty seat. This time, Kaleb took it. "By now, you have realized we are not exactly what we appear to be—I know, an understatement. You were sent here, not because you're crazy, but to see if you fit the requirements the Syndicate sets for the Army's paranormal special ops team."

"Excuse me?"

"We have recently had a few openings in the team, and, when the incident happened in Alaska, we knew it was time to get you here to assess if you were ready or able to be a member."

"So we *were* training."

"I personally would have ripped someone's head off if I'd had to attend the classes you had," Rekkus said with obvious respect.

"It's not that bad," Cyrus said without conviction.

"Deep-breathing shit? Are you kidding me? Trixie is as flaky as they come."

"Don't let Sage hear you say that, Rekkus."

Rekkus growled, and, for the first time, the growl made sense. "You've suspected for most of your life that things weren't always what they appeared. In high school, you came across a changeling on your swim team. You approached him about something not being quite right with him."

Kaleb searched his memory and pinpointed the episode, a few moments in his teenage life. The new kid at school had been acting weird one minute, fine the next. Kaleb had spent too many months training to have some drugged-up kid pretending to be an athlete ruin it for him. "I thought the kid was doping."

"Whether you thought he pretended to be someone he wasn't, or you genuinely suspected a paranormal entity, it got the attention of the Syndicate when the boy informed his father." Rekkus leaned forward, resting his elbows on his knees. "You see, most humans don't see what they aren't supposed to; their brains shut out what shouldn't be there. You, on the contrary, *do* see. Your brain questions. You knew what you had seen in school and what had been lurking under the water that night when Jim died. We have both caught you staring at the night sky here. Do the other humans see it, too? Probably, but do they believe it or simply think it's a mirage of some sort?"

"So, I've been on some fucking watch list for twenty years?"

Cyrus nodded and let Rekkus continue. "On and off. You made it easy by joining the Coast Guard, but, to be honest, until the mermaid showed her ugly head in Alaska, your file hadn't been reviewed since the initial opening."

"You said the Syndicate?"

"The paras' ruling body. They govern our kind and make the rules we live by."

"And they want me to do what?"

"I want you."

His eyebrows must have hit his hairline. He didn't think Rekkus swung that way. "Excuse me?"

"What Rekkus is saying," Cyrus said, chuckling, "is that he and, to a lesser extent, I, are charged with finding people to fill certain positions that open in Para Elite Force. The PEF makes sure that the 'normal' world is safe from paras who haven't been following the rules."

"Why don't you just get other paras to go after paras?"

"Because any para can smell me coming a mile away. You, however, blend in with the rest of your kind." Rekkus smiled, sniffing the air.

"Besides, Rekkus is too well-known amongst our kind to work undercover."

"And you?"

Cyrus appeared uncomfortable for a moment before shrugging. "I have no stomach for killing."

"The unit is based out of Salem, Massachusetts," Rekkus put in. "It's easy to hide paranormal behavior there, as most are expecting to see actors on the streets pretending to be what they aren't. But you can live anywhere you see fit. Alaska, Salem, or even here if you so choose."

"Why would I want to live here?"

"There is a certain Siren I could name."

"Yeah, let's talk about that. How much laughing did you get at my expense over her? The man who thinks he's nuts for seeing a mermaid is actually the idiot *fucking one.*"

Rekkus raised an eyebrow, but Cyrus at least had the good grace to flush. "No one laughed, believe me."

"I'm having a hard time believing anyone right now."

Rekkus's patience with the conversation seemed to be waning, "I couldn't care less about what the hell goes on with you and Serena. I need a good man to fill the shoes of another who took early retirement. So, wherever you go, is up to you. Do you want the job or not?"

"Why is there an opening?"

"Justin got shot."

"Who's Justin?"

"Justin Lawson is one of the bravest and most honorable humans either Cyrus or I know. To say he was hit by friendly fire would be a lie. There was nothing friendly about it."

Cyrus nodded in agreement. "The shooter—a member of his own team—took out his kneecap. Although they offered Justin a desk job, he refused. Not that I blame him."

"What would I be doing?"

"At the moment, we need you in rescue and recovery. We have plenty of operatives ready with skills suited to Justin's former position, and, with training, they might one day be as good as he was." Cyrus handed him a sheet of paper. "But you have other skills we could use."

He read over the job description and starting pay

then stared at the men. "This is monthly?"

Cyrus lifted his gaze to Rekkus, who shook his head. *Well, the number did seem too high.*

"Weekly," Cyrus said.

Had Kaleb been drinking, he'd have spat the liquid across the desk. Monthly, this was way more than he made, but as a *weekly* salary? "That's a lot of money."

"It's a dangerous job." Rekkus offered him a pen.

"You're very certain I'll sign."

"I don't pick people out of a hat, and I certainly don't waste my time on those not worthy of it." Rekkus stood and headed to the door, his ever-strong disposition softening a bit. "By the way, if you're angry she never told you the truth, consider two things. One, she was contractually bound with me to let no human know, and two—and I have personal experience in this—there is never a good time to tell your prospective mate you are something more than you appear. Now, if you will excuse me, I have to check on mine. But I think we should speak after dinner. By then, I am sure you'll have more questions. Shall Myron have your bags taken back to the cabin or to a room?"

"Won't her cards tell her?"

"Her cards will tell her where you should be or where you want to be, but won't tell her where you will say you want to be. Humans never do what they really want to do. Their ego gets in the way." Rekkus walked out of the room.

Kaleb leaned over the desk in front of him and banged his forehead against it. Over and over. Cyrus laughed, got up, and went to inform Myron to have Kaleb's bags returned to his cabin. And to take the cabin off the reservation list. How had they turned him leaving the island into not only staying, but signing on for a new job?

Job!

"Wait. I can't leave. I still have a tour to finish with the Coast Guard." Kaleb followed Cyrus out of the office to where Myron worked on the computer.

"You have been promoted and transferred."

"Just like that?"

"Just like that. Anything else?"

"You tell me."

Cyrus chuckled again and nudged Myron with his elbow. "Anything else?"

"Nope."

Kaleb braced himself and let his ego go for a second. "What about Serena?"

Myron placed the cards in a series of piles and flipped them over and over. Shaking her head, she swiped the number cards away in frustration. "I stopped getting a reading on her right before you came into the lobby."

When Kaleb threw the necklace into the water. Damn, he'd been impulsive. He nodded and walked out the door. He had a lot to think about. In truth, he couldn't return to his old unit. He knew that now. His world had altered, and there was no going back. But this new job seemed like a dream come true. The pay was good, it seemed custom designed for his skillset, and he would never get bored.

The after-dinner meeting took place on the porch of Rekkus's cabin, attended by Cyrus and a few of the other security guards. They told him how the Wiccan

Haus started, about Cyrus's gift as a retrocog—which Kaleb made him prove—and how Cyrus had a bounty on his head. Rekkus, being charged with keeping him safe, had also chosen to make the Wiccan Haus home—hammered into place by the Fates bringing him his mate.

To Kaleb's amazement, they even brought out the beer. And although the cold draft hit the spot, he couldn't help but gaze out over the moonlit bay. No sign at all of Serena. Yes, he had been angry—and still held on to some of it. Yes, he had been ready to walk away, but she had run first. Well, swum. Swum as far and as fast as her fin would carry her.

It didn't take long before everyone made their excuses and Kaleb, guidebook tucked under his arm, walked back to the cabin, ready to read the thing guaranteed to knock him out for the night. But he found himself unable to get into the bed he had shared with Serena, so instead, he bunked down on the sofa.

As the sun peeked over the windowsill, he realized he had spent the entire night reading. And he still had half the pages to go. There were more paras in this world than Kaleb could have imagined, and now he wondered how many he had dealt with on a regular basis.

He skipped breakfast to take a much-needed nap. Life on the island became significantly better when he didn't have to follow their rules, but could just *be*. He was lounging in a chair on the porch of Serena's cabin when Yavonka came to the beach at her usual time, but, learning of Serena's absence, she refused his offer to assist in her swimming lesson. They were in the middle of a conversation when she looked out over the water, turned white as a sheet, and bolted back up the hill. Concerned, Kaleb chased after her. Following her, he registered the shock of seeing the woman's arm, which had been amputated at the shoulder, now seemed to have grown to just above the elbow. He made a mental note to ask someone how Yavonka had managed to regrow a body part.

Entering the lobby, Kaleb watched her slip into the elevator. Even if he wanted to, he couldn't have kept following her; the second elevator only worked for paras, according to the guidebook. As seemed her way whenever she was needed, Sage appeared, walking down the hall toward him.

After alerting her that she might want to check on Yavonka, Kaleb intended to head out, but Myron stopped him. "Where's Rekkus?"

"No idea. Why?"

"Dana's in danger."

They both rounded toward the door in time to hear a tiger roar echo across the island.

Chapter Eight

Serena swam around the island, heartbroken, Kaleb's face as she had begun singing burned into her memory, the expression of devotion searing her soul. She couldn't go back and face him now. Her mother had turned her out. Serena remained adrift at sea. She *had* nowhere else to go. Bracing herself, she came in to shore when she spotted Kaleb by the water, bag over his shoulder.

He cursed her and threw something into the ocean. As soon as it hit the water, Serena knew what that something had been, their bond broken in that moment. He had thrown her tear back into the sea. She hadn't expected any less and didn't blame him for it, but it still hurt. Whatever connection they had severed, and she felt like she was bleeding out. Cemil had been right. Unlike a para, he had free choice, and he had chosen to turn her away.

She spent the rest of the night swimming. She didn't go to the other side of the island for fear the boat would be gone and so would Kaleb. Instead, she wandered around the sea floor, angering more than one lobster and picking a fight with a swordfish. But, in the end, Serena drew close to the island again. She stayed well outside the protective fog wall, not that it mattered. The wall could be penetrated easily enough underwater—the one true weakness in the island's outer defenses.

Debating whether to go through or not, Serena spent hours arguing it out in her mind. The pros and cons of never going back versus standing up and fighting for what she wanted circled in her brain. He might have left the island already, for all she knew. And, if he had departed, how would she manage the long trip to Alaska to find him.

Diving deep where the barrier was at its weakest, Serena waited on the edge. She wished the Fates would make her decision for her, one way or another. Something to tell her she belonged somewhere.

And then she felt the ripple—fear, anger, hatred—surging through the water. So much confusion and chaos near the beach. Through it all, she sensed one pure thing. Dana was scared and in the water. Bursting through the barrier, Serena ignored the sting from forging through the magic. Dana needed help.

Coming into the bay, Serena saw two sharks circling the outer edge. Serena moved quickly, calling to her sisters. She had sensed them in the waters around her last night, and they couldn't have gone far. As much as they didn't agree with how she lived her life, no mermaid would stay away with a woman in need of their help. Serena could smell the blood. Not much more than a few drops, but the sharks were getting edgy. The were-sharks in the shallows were in human form, with their pet bull sharks circling as guards in the deep water, two inside the underwater protective barrier of the island and three outside the entrance the school had used.

Serena? Serafina's voice sang in her head.

Were-sharks have attacked a woman. I can't get close enough to find out why. There are too many pets.

My favorite sport, came the voice of her youngest

sister, Orabel.

Serena moved through the water toward the circling bull sharks. They were dumb, but aggressive and mean. She needed to be careful. But she had to lead them out past the barrier. If her youngest sister swam out there, there were others. Orabel never went anywhere alone.

We have the three out here pursuing us. Now get us the ones in there, Serafina added, a bit of a smile to her voice.

Serena knew the best way to get their attention. She swam to jagged rocks in the deepest part of the alcove and pricked her finger across the sharp edge until specks of blood drifted into the water. She had been unprepared for the first bull shark ramming her in the side with its blunt snout. Shaking it off, she'd just gotten her bearings back when the second shark aimed its attack at her. Serena crested as the beast snapped its jaws. With an upshot of her tail, she knocked the bull back a few feet before diving deep again to move through the barrier. As expected, the fish followed to be sideswiped by her sisters, knocking the sharks unconscious. Two more mermaids led the animals to safe spots to avoid them flipping over.

Thank you, Serena said, heading back through the barrier *Stay close. I'll be bringing some were-sharks you don't need to be as careful with.*

We can come in and kill them there, Orabel suggested.

No, no one must die in the Wiccan Haus. Cyrus had seen too much death, and she would do what she could to keep the island a kill-free zone. If the sharks played nice.

As she swam away, she relayed her memories of her chats with Yavonka, assuring her these were-sharks would never make it much past the barrier alive. To prevent disaster from happening either by shark or tiger, she had to work fast.

Swimming close to the shore, Serena bided her time. In human form, were-sharks' senses were weak, but their bodies were strong. Rekkus paced the beach. Lifting her head just enough to assess the situation, she saw a war about to erupt. Eight were-sharks in human form guarded their alpha, who held Dana in his grasp—the same brute who had ordered Yavonka's arm removed. The asshole held a large shark's tooth to Dana's neck. Already, trickles of blood dripped down her fragile skin.

"Well, well, well, the great Rekkus. It seems we each have something the other wants. Come on, kitty, face me like a man."

Rekkus, normally never one to take an order, shifted back into human form, his rage radiating from him through the water with every step he took deeper into the surf. Serena could feel his anger growing into a storm of its own, forcing two of the were-sharks back a step. "Let go of my mate."

"You give me mine, and I will give you yours. No?"

Serena sank back under the water; too many people on the beach now, someone would spot her and give away her presence. She could still hear the conversation, but one of the un-shifted weres had moved deeper into the water. She could sing to an unmated were and affect him. Coming up behind him, she hummed softly so only he could hear. He tried to struggle, but her song stayed the shift, leaving him defenseless and human. Luring him along, she used her powers to allow him to breathe—something she had never done before. These powers were ingrained in her as a mermaid, but Serena had never used them, too frightened she might kill someone. Now, it didn't matter if these weres died. After what they had put Yavonka through, and the fear they were causing Dana, her family could have at them. Keeping the were entranced, she led him to her waiting sisters.

Seven more.

Kaleb stood behind Rekkus, waiting for the word for him to strike. Rekkus focused on the creature with his wife. But Kaleb and Cyrus watched the others around them. Lakshmi, the massage therapist, had shown up and shifted into her golden lioness form— that should have surprised him, but it didn't. Sage and Sarka had stayed back to ensure Yavonka wouldn't come down and put more people in danger. Cemil, at the other end of the beach, headed off anyone who came that way.

"Weren't there eight of them?" Kaleb whispered.

Cyrus nodded and glanced to the side for a split second. Following the direction of Cyrus's gaze, Kaleb saw her. Serena. She swam up, got the nearest man-shark's attention, and, within seconds, the man disappeared. Kaleb shuddered to think where. But the numbers were even. Six to six.

"Perhaps, tiger, my aim is in the wrong place." Dana's eyes grew wide as her captor moved the tooth from her throat to her abdomen. "Perhaps if I threatened to remove your cubs and feed them to my pets, that would motivate you to bring what is mine."

All hell broke loose. Rekkus shifted and lunged at the shark's neck. Rekkus and Dana fell in the water with the were-shark with a splash, while the other sharks moved onshore, each going on the attack. Their goal seemed to be getting to the Haus to get their alpha's mate. Kaleb didn't take his eyes off the man, strong as he might seem, this big freak before him didn't have a brain cell to spare.

"You might be king of the sea, but this is land,

asshole," Kaleb said as the creature with fists the size of blacksmith's mallets moved in to pulverize him. The were-shark might be slow and awkward, but if the man hit his mark, he'd put a hurting on Kaleb.

He managed to out maneuver, until, finally, the taller man paused for air. Kaleb punched him in the chest, following with a roundhouse kick to the face. The man gaped at Kaleb for a minute before his eyes rolled into his head and he fell with a *thump*.

Kaleb took in the chaos surrounding him. Everyone available fought off the invaders. One of the Wiccan Haus guards severely injured still fought with the strength of a bear, and the other did her best to fight off the were-shark coming at her. The Rowan brothers were holding their own, and there were more were-animals fighting the "sharks" than he had been aware were on the island.

In the distance, one of the thugs tried to sneak up on Rekkus, not something that would work if his attention weren't on his wife. Kaleb was about to jump in when a large tail came out of the water and smacked the shark almost hard enough to knock his head off.

Serena surfaced, and she pointed to the lioness by the treeline. "Help Lakshmi."

Kaleb turned to see the lioness backed into a corner. Her dark eyes were the same in both human and lion form. Grabbing a piece of driftwood, Kaleb hauled off and swung at her aggressor. One strike took him down, the board cracking in two.

Only then did he see Cyrus helping Dana from the water, the cut bleeding into her cotton dress in contrast to her pale skin. Any minute she would pass out. Rekkus and the shark leader were nowhere to be found. The water became eerily quiet for the next few seconds as everyone seemed to hold their breath. Then Rekkus materialized in human form, hitting the water with a fist. "Damn it!"

"Get out of there!" Cemil yelled.

The warning came too late. Everyone saw the gigantic dorsal fin surface with the caudal fin swishing behind. Rekkus closed his eyes, bracing for the impact. What happened next seemed to play out in slow motion. The shark rammed into Rekkus, thrusting him through the water as the big man beat the shark on the head. But just as Rekkus was dragged under, two mermaids jumped out of the water like dolphins in an amusement park show and dove back in. Serena, and the other Kaleb recognized from the lake the day before. The water churned, frothing pink with blood. Kaleb stormed waist-deep into the water before he knew it. The only sounds seeping in were Dana's screams to get free of Cyrus and back to Rekkus.

Swimming full speed toward the war happening underwater, Kaleb worked through the commotion only to have the water go flat calm. Turning, he scanned the cove but saw nothing—no shark, no tiger, and no mermaids. He faced the beach and shook his head, trying to block out the cries of despair from Dana. Sage and Sarka raced down the path at full speed.

The quiet seemed to stretch forever until, finally, Rekkus emerged next to him, gasping for air. Kaleb wrapped an arm around the man, who was bleeding but conscious.

"Don't fight me." Kaleb dragged Rekkus back against his chest.

"Can't—"

As he worked the two of them into the shallows, he kept scanning the water, hoping and praying to see two mermaids crest again. Cemil and Cyrus grabbed Rekkus, who did no more than take a few steps before collapsing at his mate's feet, blood pouring out of his leg from the shark's bite. Dana fell to her knees, hysterical. But Rekkus placed a hand with spread fingers on her belly and pulled her head down. "You. Haven't. Seen. Smothering. Yet."

A relieved laugh came from Dana, who broke down in a sea of tears all over again.

Kaleb turned to scan the water. Serena crested, spinning in the air before diving back in. Kaleb stood at the ocean's edge as she approached. As she switched from swimming to walking, her fins disappeared and her legs split, a dress covering her as though the ocean had created it.

She was so beautiful.

She rushed to him, touching him all over as if

looking for injuries. "Are you okay?"

"Me? I wasn't the one luring sharks away one by one," he grated out before surrounding her in his embrace. "I'm okay now."

"Dana?"

"Seems fine, but will never have a minute's peace again."

Kaleb put his arm around Serena and led her to where Rekkus and Dana sat still on the beach, covered in blankets, Rekkus's head in Dana's lap. Sage packed the wound with herbs and wrapped his leg the best she could with him still lying down.

"So, when were you planning to announce the happy news?" Sage demanded, a hint of actual anger in her voice.

"God, if *he* was smothering me, why would I tell the whole island? I could barely breathe as it was," Dana said, but her voice held no conviction, not anymore. And Kaleb understood. She had felt safe here, and now she didn't. Although she had mated with a were-tiger, she had never grasped the danger it entailed. "I am so sorry, Rekkus."

"Shhhh, give me a few hours and I will be good as new." Rekkus motioned for Kaleb and Serena to come forward.

"Thank you, both of you. I owe you my life. And, more important, I owe my mate's life and our unborn cubs to you, too."

"It's what I do," Serena said, too choked up to add anything else, but she teetered on the edge of a breaking point, and Kaleb held her closer. "My sisters have taken the sharks far away. They will deal out justice, so you won't have to."

Rekkus nodded, as he drifted into a healing sleep. Within a few seconds, his shift happened, leaving the large tiger in the human's place.

"Damn, ain't no moving him now," Cyrus cursed as he started to gather wood. "We need to build a fire to keep him warm."

"We'll need to cast the circle, too. I need everyone not picking up sticks to grab as many stones as possible," Sarka ordered as she placed rocks around the couple.

Serena passed a few to Cemil who smiled and set

them where they needed to be. For the next few minutes, all worked together until a ring of stones surrounded the tiger and his lady.

Sarka held the last of the stones. "Cyrus, in."

"What?"

"Get your ass in the circle."

"Excuse me?"

Sage stepped forward. "We're weak without Rekkus, and someone may know that. You'll be safe within the protection of the stones."

"And Rekkus won't truly enter the healing sleep if he's worried about you," Cemil added, nudging Cyrus forward.

Once he'd entered the circle, Sarka placed the last rock and began chanting.

"What if I have to pee, damn it?"

Still chanting, Sarka tossed him a cup.

"Are you kidding me?" Cyrus, who had never lost his cool in the time Kaleb had been on the island, took two steps forward, hit the ring barrier, and fell on his ass. "So help me, Sarka, when you let me out of here…."

Kaleb had no wish to watch any more of the lunacy. Rekkus lay unconscious next to the bonfire, Dana curled next to him, petting him. Kaleb could see her shoulders shaking and knew she cried tears she didn't wish anyone to see. Cyrus circled the bonfire, hunting for a flaw in the ring. All while cursing his sister. The rest of the siblings and a few more staff members had joined in the chanting, and Kaleb and Serena were no longer needed.

He needed to wrap his arms around her, feel her against him. Everything had changed in a matter of forty-eight hours. Serena, a mermaid he had believed to be a monster, had put her life at risk to help people who didn't like them, all to save a woman in danger. Not the act of a monster, but the act of a hero. He drew her toward their cabin, where they could be alone.

She stopped. "You don't hate me?"

"I love you."

"But…."

Her eyes swirled with life. He understood so much now. Missing pieces fit into place. "There is no 'but.' It's that simple."

Kaleb could feel her sadness, almost as if it were his own. She glanced toward the sea. "You threw the tear away."

He sighed, loosening his arm around her waist. "I acted in anger. The world as I knew it had shifted on its axis, and I went a bit crazy. If I could find your tear, I would never take it off again." He stepped away from her, scanning the bay where so much had happened and where he had thrown her gift in a fit of rage. One he only now fully appreciated.

"Perhaps the tides haven't taken it yet. You threw it out here?" Serena put up a finger in a gesture for him to wait. She took only a few steps in when another mermaid emerged from the dark water and made her way toward them. "Serafina? What is it?"

"We didn't say farewell, and I wanted to meet your man." Serafina eyed her sister the same way Kaleb's family did. Warmth and protection, mixed with a good deal of compassion. Serafina smiled at him before turning back to her sister with expectation.

"Serafina, please meet Kaleb, the most honorable

man I have ever met. Kaleb, this is my oldest sister, Serafina."

Kaleb nodded but maintained his distance. One of the things Cyrus had insisted on teaching him the night before had been the best ways to stay safe with a mermaid in the area. Step one, always carry earplugs. Failed step one. Step two, never get near the water. Passed step two. And step three, never, ever, get involved in a fight between mermaids. That made sense—any man knew not to get in the middle of ladies fighting. "It's a pleasure to meet you, Serafina."

Serafina assessed him up and down and turned to her sister, brow furrowed. "Are you sure?"

"More sure than I have ever been in my existence. I'm finally living."

Serafina smiled. The same grin Serena had, but without the sucker-punch effect hers always hit him with. "Then I think he might have lost this." Holding out the necklace with the sea glass, she put it in Serena's palm. "Take care of her for us. She's the special one."

"I plan to."

"Good." Serafina nodded toward the bonfire on the beach. "I'm going to let them know where we have taken the sharks. The alpha is dead. As you asked, we made sure not to kill him within the barriers of the island. He wouldn't have made it much longer anyway. The tiger had hit a major artery. Much to the great disappointment of Orabel whose bloodlust knows no bounds, but in the end, his life-force left him far from here."

"Thank you for that," Serena said, knowing they had no reason to follow her request other than love for her.

"I will miss you, sister."

Serena hugged her good-bye one more time before turning to give Kaleb his necklace back. "I will ask Sarka to fix the clasp in the morning."

"I should have trusted you and my gut. Instead, I let my ego and my anger overrule my instincts."

She lifted his fist to her mouth, kissing his knuckles. "I don't blame you for being angry. I would have been angry myself."

"I was afraid you would never come back."

"I was afraid you had left."

Brushing his lips against her forehead, he led her into the cabin and closed the door. "I'm not leaving. They offered me a job, and I took it."

"Here? I don't understand."

He laughed. "No, not here exactly. More all over the place. But I can make my home here if you want. I have family in Alaska, but, now that I know better, I don't think Alaska is a good fit for us. I understand the water may be a bit too cold."

She blushed. "But I can't stay *here* forever."

"I think if you talk to the siblings, they have something figured out." Stifling a yawn, Kaleb turned off the lights in the front room. "But, tonight, if it's all the same to you, I would like to take a hot shower and go to sleep with my arms wrapped around you."

"Just sleep?"

"God, do you paras ever run out of energy?" It felt weird to say *para,* but Kaleb figured it would get easier with time.

She laughed, kissing him softly on the lips.

"Sleep sounds like a nice idea. I still can't believe you don't hate me."

"I can't believe you're a deadly Siren. I wish you'd told me the truth, but I suppose the bigger the secret, the harder it is to let someone know. And I can't blame a whole race because of what one individual did, now can I?"

Her voice full of passion, she said, "I love so you much it hurts."

"Perhaps, tomorrow, when I have some energy, I can love you so much it feels good."

Standing under the stream of the shower, Kaleb kissed Serena with every bit of emotion he had and swore he would never let her go again.

Chapter Nine

Serena awoke long before dawn. Kaleb's light snores filled the room as she took a last glance at him before leaving the cabin. The sun had yet to peek over the horizon, but she needed to do so much. The beach stood empty, the only evidence of the events the day before the dying embers of the bonfire, although two security guards remained on either side of the door to Rekkus's cabin. They acknowledged her with a slight nod, but said nothing.

The island was at its most peaceful, long before the humans woke. The vampires had all settled in for the day, and, except for the sounds of the waves on the beach, everything waited quietly for dawn to arrive. As she reached the top of the hill, Serena watched the sunrise reaching fire-colored fingers into the morning sky.

To her surprise, Myron sat at the front desk, an hour before her usual shift started. Myron smiled as she put on whatever name tag she'd found in the drawer. *Tina* today. "Sage is in the office. She would like to talk to you."

Prepared for this, Serena took a deep breath and went in. Sage sat at the desk, yawning against the back of her fingers. She smiled and waved Serena to sit as she leaned her head against the wall. "I can't believe you're up so early."

"I don't need a lot of sleep."

"Well, I do. But I need to wait until Cemil wakes before I can take a nap."

"Myron said you wanted to see me?"

"Yes, I hoped Cyrus and Rekkus would be here to talk with you, too. But I think they're raiding the kitchen."

"Rekkus is up?"

"And a sourer mood I have never seen. But I suppose it's to be expected. His pregnant wife was nearly kidnapped by sharks. He's limping, but I'm sure will be right as rain by evening." She yawned again. "Anyway, I hope you don't think me too forward, but Kaleb has requested his home base be here on the island. We don't usually allow that, but for the two of you, we'll make the exception. We would love to have you join our staff."

"You want me to work here?"

"Yes. We thought you could assist with hydro-therapy. Yavonka still needs you—"

"And I need someone on security to deal with the underwater threats, as well as help track that odd rip current offshore," Rekkus said, limping into the office. "You're the obvious choice."

"I don't understand. Aren't you worried I might hurt someone?"

Sage shook her head. "The only person at risk of being hurt by you is Kaleb. And he seems willing to take the risk."

"So?" Rekkus asked with a knowing smile.

She nodded. "When Kaleb isn't on missions, he can come back here?"

"Through the portal," Sage acknowledged.

"Am I allowed to sing?"

"Don't push your luck," Rekkus said, but no bite trailed with his words.

An hour later, Serena walked out of the office

with an amazed sense of purpose to her life. Myron remained focused on her cards, but murmured her welcome. She found Kaleb in the dining hall, devouring eggs, bacon, and sausage, with an empty plate beside his full one. She hadn't thought about the fact that everyone had missed dinner the evening before, but this had been one of those times where it couldn't be helped.

As Serena approached, Kaleb stood, kissed her, and then returned his focus to his food. She watched him eat while waiting for her meal, feeling a new peace. He knew her true self and didn't care. He'd seen her worst and loved her anyway. He chose to be with her. It was a powerful revelation.

Finishing the last of his eggs, he sat back. "Sorry, starving. Where were you?"

"I am now a staff member of the Wiccan Haus."

"Congratulations, honey." He leaned forward and kissed her again, this time letting his lips linger.

"You knew."

"I had a suspicion."

"You did? I didn't."

"Marry me."

Serena looked up, her mouth forming an O.

"It can't be that shocking. When two people love each other, they get married."

"But—" Serena's heart swelled. She wanted to say yes, wanted to be his until forever. By Poseidon's crown, she wanted it more than anything. "I can't marry you."

"I know all about your reasons not to. Cyrus filled me in. I know you're afraid of killing me. I know you can't have a baby with me unless you take my soul for the baby. I know you're two hundred years old at least—which, by the way, makes you a serious cougar—"

"I am not a were-cougar." Why would he think she held a shifter gene?

"Cougar, honey, is a lady much older than the man she's with."

"That's a silly name."

"You're getting us off track here. I know all the cons. But the only thing that matters to me is the pro." He cupped her cheeks, forcing her to meet his eyes. "I love you. That is all the matters."

"I can't." Serena felt the day's brightness fade with that declaration. "I love you too much to do that to you."

"I won't give up."

"But you don't need to marry me."

"No, but I want to. I want to bring my family here to the island to meet you and get to know you, and I want to see you wearing a wedding ring on your finger that tells everyone you're mine."

Serena's food came, and Kaleb released her from his embrace to let her eat. He didn't seem mad or frustrated, just determined, and that scared Serena more than anything else.

So a pattern started at breakfast, lunch, and dinner. Kaleb would propose, and Serena would refuse. Until the night before he was set to deploy for the first time. Both had been quiet that evening. Serena was nervous about his coming assignment. Not that she had a clue what it involved, but he would be gone for a month. Kaleb had requested that they be allowed to dine alone at their cabin, since neither of them were guests of the Haus anymore.

She had lined up as many people to work with the next day as possible. Kaleb would be leaving via the portal in the morning, and each second of the clock mocked her like a cruel reminder. When they got the part of the meal where he always popped the question, he remained silent. Pensive, even, and a sadness that perhaps he had given up on asking filled her. She ate the food, but it tasted like sand. The soft music playing in the background grated on her nerves.

She found him standing over her, hand outstretched. "Come with me."

"Where?"

"Don't question, just come with me."

She let him lead her out to the water's edge. "No."

He stripped down to his skin. The only thing he kept on was her tear. "You have never hurt me, and I don't think you ever would. Why can't you have the faith in you that I have? Just a swim."

As she watched him walk into the water under

the full moon, his well-sculpted back and ass disappearing under the dark seawater, Serena closed her eyes and searched for the willpower to say no. She had used that word so often it seemed to be the only one she said. But, this time, she couldn't find it. She needed this; she needed him. So, taking the step to follow him, she let the water surround her as it always did, letting it come alive around her before diving in. Feeling the water glide over skin that turned to scales and feet that merged into a fin, she surfaced next to him.

His smile drove her crazy with the need to kiss him. "Show me what you are."

"What?"

"I trust you. Show me your world. Show me the world I could never see without you."

"I am so scared of hurting you. I'm scared…."

"Shhh. No fears. Just show me. I want to know everything about who you are."

She nodded, letting him pull her toward him. They had never been this close in the water. She had always kept him at a distance when she was in mermaid form. His hands ran down her back, over her scale-covered backside, and he looked up at her, shocked. "The scales. They're so smooth, like glass. I didn't expect that."

" Wait you haven't seen anything yet," she said and smiled. She brought her lips to his and let her tongue play with his full bottom lip. "Take a deep breath."

He did, and, as Serena kissed him hard, he fought for air for a second as she took them under the water. She broke the kiss and blew an air bubble at him that surrounded his nose and mouth. Excitement filling her, she tightened her hold on him and swam off, leading him to the opening of the island's barrier.

Some whales in the distance, heading to their mating grounds in the warmer waters, were resting for the night. Kaleb's eyes widened as they paused a few feet from them. The big mammals did no more than blink at Serena and Kaleb, knowing they were no threat. Swimming a little deeper into the ocean, Serena shared the life around them.

Telepathically, she told him of the turtles to the

east, the school of swordfish that headed deep out to sea, and the mermaid in the distance who thought she was being stealthy even though Serena could sense her a league away. But then he turned to her, all sense of fun gone as he urged her to the water's surface. "Sing to me, Siren. Sing me a song."

"Kaleb, I can't."

"You can, and then we're going to make love, and I am going to prove to you that you aren't going to kill me."

"I can't. Please don't ask this of me." She turned away, tears filling her eyes. "I just can't."

"I trust you. Myron even agreed this is the only way. She says the number three has been surrounding me since I arrived. Perhaps the three meant three battles I needed to go through. One, your mother, two, the sharks, three, your demons. Sarka has her doubts. And Rekkus, he thinks I'm nuts."

"How many people did you tell you were going to have sex with me tonight?"

He threw his head back and laughed. "I think you'll find since I already love you, your Siren's serenade will have no effect on me."

Serena took a deep breath. Should she lull him into a trance like before, she would take him back to the island, and this would all be done. She wouldn't have to worry about him doing this again. But—and it was a big but—what if he was right? What if....

Come, men of the land,

Come and meet me on the strand.

Your hearts they grow weary, and my eyes are all teary,

For the man I need is away on the sea.

Come, men of the land,

Come walk in the sand.

Your soul is now mine, and like the fish on your line,

The man that I need is now one with the sea.

She finished singing and waited, watching as Kaleb stared at her for a moment before blinking and saying with a smile, "Yours is the most beautiful voice I have ever heard, and if you need to take me all this way out to sea for me to hear it, I will come every time."

"It didn't work?"

"Of course not, silly."

"Why did it work before?"

"Cemil has a theory that, when you sang to me the last time, while I thought I might have loved you, I didn't know who or what you were. So I couldn't be truly in love with you. Now I know you, secrets and all, and still I love you. So you can't enthrall me with your song."

That made sense, and it gave her strength to move on to the next part of his plan. "I am not sure how this works, exactly. I have never dragged a man down to the depths to have sex with him."

"Well, that's nice to know. I'm sure we'll figure it out," Kaleb said, but his voice caught. For all his tough guy posturing, his nerves were raw. But he took this chance for her. "But when this is all said and done, I am going to ask you to marry me one last time. And you are going to say yes, understand?"

She nodded and would have said more, but his mouth descended on hers, his kiss punishing and passionate rolled into one. Her head spun, and, had they been on land, he would have swept her off her feet. But they were at sea, and the Siren within her took over.

Serena spun them in a circle until they were fully submerged. Never breaking apart, they kissed as they sank to the sea floor. She leaned back, her body tingling, and when she let out a breath, she created a bubble that surrounded them both. The water receded from the bubble, and her scaled fin disappeared until she lay naked beside Kaleb.

Reaching up, he kissed her again, trailing his lips down her neck, over her collarbone, and to the first pert nipple he came to. His palm caressed the other until he could lavish it with the same attention as the first. He shifted her beneath him, onto the soft, fine sand, careful to swipe away any shells or debris. He didn't say a word—not that she expected him to. No sounds came from them or the ocean around them. Just serene silence.

Kaleb didn't stop his descent at her breast but continued down over her stomach to nibble on her hip. He eased back to see her sprawled open to him, grinning before placing one of her legs on his shoulder and nudging her other leg to the side. He stared down at her, and she in awe of how passionately he looked at her, could take her eyes off him. He eased down to her apex, his tongue working over her clit, each stroke making it harder to breathe. The air rushed from her lungs as her legs started to shake. Serena supported herself on unsteady elbows, wanting to watch every minute of him feasting upon her.

After her orgasm overtook her, and after the shaking had eased, Kaleb stopped his assault. His eyes burned into her, never leaving her face as he got to his knees. Still coming down from the climax, Serena didn't fight him when he engulfed her in his embrace and drove his cock deep inside her. He kneaded her ass as he controlled the rhythm. Over and over, he pulled out to thrust back in her, until she could take no more and fractured all over again in his arms. Pants and cries lay silent in the abyss; not a sound could be heard.

He quickened his pace. Kaleb had never been this

frenzied before; laying her and driving into her, he seemed harder, larger. Serena dug her heels into the sand and met his thrusts, trying to help him achieve the orgasm he strove for. For what seemed like eons, they moved each other closer while still easing apart. Until, as his seed rushed into her womb and drained him of his energy, the bubble around them burst. Water rushed in, and Kaleb, unable to move, pinned her to the sand, her legs apart and unable to mold into her fin.

He looked at her through the dark water for a brief second before his eyes closed. Panicked, she shoved at him, Serena let out a high-pitch screech as he fell unconscious on her shoulder. She could feel the life draining from Kaleb and struggled, frantic to get out from under him.

No, not like this, not now....

And as she had gave up all hope, fingers wrapped around her arm, helping her out from under Kaleb. Free, her legs fused instantly. Serena turned to try to fight off whoever tried to attack.

Her mother, in all her beauty, smiled. "Go. Take

him up above."

With a shove from her mother, not caring if it was too quick for his body to take, she moved them forward, faster and faster until she broke the surface like a killer whale, pulling him with her into the air, landing with a smack on the water.

Kaleb was shocked out of his trance, coughing up water and gasping for air all at once.

"Oh, thank Poseidon."

Kaleb floated on his back, taking deep breaths into his lungs. Serena helped, holding him above water. She sensed her mother behind her. Turning, Serena prepared herself for a fight, but there appeared no fight in her mother, just a funny kind of sadness.

"Mother, why? Why did you help me save him? You could have gotten everything you wanted."

"Because his soul would never have been your baby's."

"I don't understand. He was seconds from death."

"It's because my soul belongs to you." Kaleb lowered himself into a treading-water position.

"Kaleb?"

"You're my soul mate. Any babe of ours can't take a soul already given."

Serena looked to him, and then to her mother, who nodded. "I wish you only happiness, my daughter, and perhaps, when you are ready to ascend to the throne, you will be a more open-minded queen than I."

"I have no interest in your throne."

"That's good to know, as I have no interest in abdicating anytime soon. Now, if you will excuse me, I will leave you to take him back home. And may I suggest, in the future, when you desire to mate at the bottom of the ocean, let her be on top." She disappeared as quickly as she had appeared.

"Let's go home. You wore me out," Kaleb said with a wicked grin.

Serena laughed before kissing him in a verification he still lived. She was finally free to love him as she wanted to love him. She felt free to be herself. And as they swam side by side back to the island, she sang to him of love and joy.

Reaching the beach, Kaleb stopped her when she would have walked straight inside the cabin. Getting down on one knee, he gazed up at her.

"Serena, will you marry me?"

For the first time in her life, Serena did what she wanted to. She said yes.

Epilogue

Five years later....

From her seated position on the beach, Serena caught sight of her husband walking down the path to their cabin. He paused only for a second before picking up the pace. It had been three months since he had last been home. Moving on feet that had a mind of their own, Serena ran and threw herself into his arms. Luckily, he'd braced himself, or the two of them would have ended up horizontal on the ground. And horizontal almost always meant naked.

Dropping his bag, Kaleb picked her up into his arms and carried her. Cocking his head to the side, he listened for a moment. "Where's Coral?"

"Your daughter is swimming in the lake with Dana and the cubs."

"Do you think that's safe?" he asked, moving into protective-father mode. It never ceased to amaze her that the second he was home, he forgot she had managed without him all those months.

She stepped back, hands on her hips. "You don't give Coral enough credit. Your daughter is a damned good swimmer, and you know that. Hell, she swims better than either of us."

Easing her back into his arms, he laughed. "Silly woman. I worried about the cubs' well-being, not our daughter."

"Oh. Well...."

Kissing her into silence, Kaleb led her to their bedroom. Both cabins had received remodeling as the families had grown. Though it hadn't happened the first night in the sea, Serena did get pregnant a few months later, right after they had been officially married by Cemil on the island. Kaleb's parents had made it, as had Serafina. Her mother, still being banned from the island, had agreed it would be best to stay away.

His family had taken the news about Serena's true nature far better than either of them had expected and had welcomed her, fins and all. His parents lamented but understood when Kaleb explained the difficulty travel to Alaska would pose as no one knew for sure what effect flying would have on Serena, but they had agreed to come to the island when they could. And Serena, now quite good at using the computer, had promised to keep them up-to-date on their lives.

Although Kaleb would have liked to have been present for his wife's labor, the powers that be had decided, to ensure his safety, he had to be elsewhere. No man in all recorded history had managed to get a mermaid pregnant and still been around to meet their child. And even with Sage, Myron, and eventually Sarka's demands he leave, only when Serena begged him did he leave. Like a man waiting outside a hospital room, he'd waited on the other side of the portal. Even knowing the portal wouldn't open until sunset, he'd paced.

And although he had missed her birth, he had been there to watch Coral's first swim. He had witnessed Serena, carrying their child, walk into the bay shortly after delivery. She had placed the child in the water, and, as he waded next to them, his newborn daughter's legs merged and she swam not far from her protective mother, crying to be picked up after but a minute.

Kaleb turned out to be a natural parent, and when he lifted his mermaid daughter from the water and placed her in his loving arms unfazed by her scales and fin, Serena fell in love with him all over again.

"As much as I miss our daughter, I have missed you more."

"You know, Dana said she would keep her tonight for us."

"Perhaps we can get her after dinner." Laying Serena on the bed, Kaleb smiled. "Or perhaps we should make it breakfast."

And as he stripped naked and joined her, Serena murmured, "Welcome home, my love."

"Show me how much you missed me. Sing, my Siren."

And she sang in every way he could make her.

About the Author

Award-winning author Dominique Eastwick grew up a US Navy Brat, so if there was a naval base, that was probably home. She currently resides in North Carolina with her husband, two children, crazy lab and lazy cat.

Dominique's love of reading started when she was told to read *To Kill a Mockingbird* in high school—a book that opened her eyes to the joys of reading and entering into the world of the author. To this day she ranks this book as her favorite.

Also by Dominique:

Strawberry Kisses

The Duke and the Virgin

The Marquis and the Mistress

The Earl and His Virgin Countess

Shifting Hearts

Healing His Soul's Mate